Say I Don't

Misty Hollow, Book 7

Cynthia Hickey

Copyright © **2022 Cynthia Hickey**
Published by: Winged Publications

**This book is a work of fiction.
Names, characters, places, and incidents
are the product of the author's imagination
and are used fictitiously. Any resemblance
to actual events, locales, or persons, living
or dead, is coincidental.**

**No part of this book may be copied or
distributed without the author's consent.**

All rights reserved.

ISBN: 978-1-956654-65-3

DEDICATION

To all those who love a good page turner.

Chapter One

Gemma Ricca smiled at her reflection in the mirror. A faint sheen glowed from the wedding dress she wore. A simple bun adorned her hair. Her smile faded as once again doubts about marrying Anthony Moreno surfaced. Could she spend the rest of her life as a cherished possession? Because that's what she felt like most of the time. One more thing Anthony owned.

With a sigh she moved to the large plate window, shoved it open, and leaned on the sill to catch a breeze and gaze at the thick wooded scenery.

The Morenos had wanted an exclusive wedding, closed to the public and reporters. She shrugged. That was fine with her.

From the window, she watched Anthony and his father, also named Anthony, stroll down a path by the log cabin that was as far from a normal log cabin as it could be. Large and sprawling, the home of a Moreno relative in upstate New York made a beautiful location for a wedding. No expense had been spared.

"You're next in line, Junior." Anthony's father's voice drifted toward her as he clapped him on the shoulder. "Now that you're getting married, it's time you prove to the family that you have what it takes to run the business."

"What do I need to do?" Anthony squared his shoulders, more handsome in his tux than a man had a right to be. The sun tinted his dark hair with blue lights. He hitched his carved-in-stone jawline.

"You need to get rid of the oldest Esposito son. No need to dispose of the body. Word needs to spread that you are stepping into my shoes."

"What if my wife finds out?"

"We don't tell our wives any of our business. Their job is to do what they're told, look pretty, and give us sons. Anything more than that, and they'll be punished. Keep control of your household, son. Can you do that?"

"Absolutely." He glanced at the house.

Gemma clapped a hand over her mouth and stepped behind the curtain. Anthony was going to murder someone? Her blood chilled. What kind of family business did the Morenos own? She'd been told they'd made their money in sales.

Gemma dropped to a stuffed ottoman. She was marrying into the mob? No, she couldn't. Her hand rested on her stomach where her unborn baby was no bigger than a kidney bean. She wouldn't raise her child to take over this business someday.

A quick glance at the clock showed half an hour until the ceremony. She'd have to leave now. Gemma glanced around the room. Her suitcase full of expensive clothes would have to stay. Without a car, she would have to flee through the woods in hopes of finding someone to give her a ride. She'd worry about clothes when she arrived at her apartment.

Fortunately, she'd kept her apartment with his good wishes, although she lived with Anthony. A woman needed her own space, he'd said, but that would end when they got married. Everything in her apartment had been packed up ready to be given away or brought to the mansion. All she had to do was grab her safe, a box of clothes, and the old address book which was all she had left of her mother.

Anthony wouldn't know anything was amiss until she didn't show up for the ceremony and someone came to check on her. That gave her a thirty-minute head start. It was enough.

She peered out the door. The hallway was empty. With no family or friends to speak of, her room was crowded with bridesmaids and friends. No, the *women* assigned the task of being her bridesmaids chattered together in another room, wanting nothing to do with the woman who would take Anthony Moreno off the market.

She slipped off her shoes and stepped into the hall. A shrill laugh rang out from the bridesmaids' room. One of those women was more than welcome to her fiancé.

Where would she go? She vaguely remembered mention of an aunt, her mother's sister.

She bit the inside of her lip and tiptoed down the back stairs and out a side door. Caterers, the florist, and a bartender milled around, some of them smoking cigarettes. Gemma flashed a grin and headed down a dirt path strewn with leaves as if it were a natural thing for a bride to do on her wedding day.

Once out of sight of the house, she hitched up her gown and sprinted as fast as her bare feet would allow. No way a rock would dare be on a path owned by a Moreno. Gemma had no idea where the path led, only that it headed away from the house. *God, please let it lead to a road.*

A stitch stabbed at her side. She stopped and leaned against a tree to rest. So much for using the home gym five days a week. Breath easing, she straightened.

Her veil tangled in a low tree branch. She pulled it from her head letting it sway as a beacon to freedom.

She burst through a thick growth of bushes.

A horn blared as a car missed her by less than a foot. The car screeched to a halt. A red-faced man stuck his head out the window. "Are you crazy?"

"Please. I need your help." Gemma approached the car. "I need a ride into town. Please."

His eyes roamed from her dirty bare feet to the soiled hem of her wedding gown to her expensively made-up face. "Climb in. Can't say as I blame you for fleeing your wedding considering who you were about to wed."

"You know who I am?"

"Sweetheart, everyone in the state of New York knows who you are. Where to?"

She gave him the address and slouched in her seat. The path to freedom would be harder than she'd thought.

"Do you have any money?" The man asked.

"Yes." Thankfully, she'd kept her inheritance in an account separate from Anthony's.

"You'd best take it out of the bank before Moreno finds out you're gone."

The man was right. One more thing to do before she could leave town. "Can you drive faster? I don't have a lot of time."

The man drove her to town where she hired another man to drive her into the city. He dropped her in front of the elevator in the parking garage and wished her luck.

Gemma rode to the third floor, receiving several curious glances as she darted for her apartment. She gathered the gown around her then slammed the door behind her once she was inside. Fifteen minutes later, dressed in jeans and a long-sleeved sweater, she had her safe and a large suitcase in hand.

Back in the garage, she tossed everything into the trunk of her car before driving to the bank. She wasn't able to withdraw all her money—no bank carried that much—but she was able to withdraw fifty thousand, and have the rest held until she opened another account somewhere else.

Her heart stopped when she glanced at the clock. She'd already been gone from the wedding location for several hours. Anthony would know she'd left. Hopefully, he'd think she'd return. The man's arrogance wouldn't allow him to believe otherwise. Not at first anyway.

She put the cash in the safe in the trunk of her Cadillac, slid back in the car, and opened her mother's address book. Someone had updated an address since her mother's death. Her nanny, Rosa, perhaps? The elderly woman had warned Gemma not to marry Anthony, but the stars in her eyes had blinded her, much as the tears threatened to now. Rosa had written in the address to a place in Misty Hollow, Arkansas. She'd somehow known Gemma might need it someday.

She put the address into her GPS and headed toward her new home. Hopefully, a place she could start fresh where nobody knew, or cared, who she was.

With her hair stuffed under a baseball cap, she bought a pair of oversized sunglasses at a truck stop, so no one gave her a second glance when she stopped for gas or to catch a few hours of sleep in her car before continuing. She ate fast food and had never felt freer in her life.

Bless Nanny Rosa. With her mother's death at Gemma's birth, her father had withdrawn into himself, leaving Rosa to raise his child, thinking a healthy trust fund could suffice for his parental duties. Then, Gemma had gone off to a prestigious college, groomed for the privileged life of a rich girl and met Anthony Moreno. How things had changed. Now, at the age of twenty-five, she found herself pregnant and on the run.

She laughed. Running from the mob shouldn't feel freeing, but now no one was waiting on her, advising her how to dress, and telling her what to eat. Yes indeed, she felt very free.

Less than three days later, she approached the Ozark Mountains, lush green against a bright blue sky. Hope leaped in her chest. No one had caught up to her, and her new home was only a few hours away.

She crossed the Arkansas border and turned to climb a mountain. The Cadillac's engine purred despite the steep incline. Off to her right, she caught the occasional glimpse of a small river. Beautiful.

She turned a sharp curve at the bottom.

A deer darted into the road.

Gemma screamed and jerked the wheel.

In a flash, the car plunged over a small cliff, plowed down saplings as it sped downhill, then landed with a splash into the swiftly moving water.

Gemma lowered the window and climbed out before the water could fill the car. She grappled to hold on to the door frame, but the swift-moving water yanked her away and into the bank, only to grab her again and pull her deeper into the current.

She opened her mouth to scream for help only to take in water. The taste of marine vegetation and fish filled her mouth. She raised her head heavenward. "Help!" The water pulled her down, closing over her head.

Had she left Anthony only to die before living— truly living for the first time? "Help!" *God, please.*

She grasped for a low tree branch. Her fingers brushed the leaves as she passed.

Her limbs grew heavy. Her strength ebbed, and she went under again. "Help." She swallowed more water. Heavy coughing wracked her lungs.

Standing on the shore in the distance, a man fly-fished.

Gemma caught sight of his wide eyes as she floated past. She stretched out her arm. Please.

He dropped his pole and raced down the bank alongside her. "Hold on. I'll get you out."

She couldn't. She submerged again, not having the strength to claw her way up. Gemma relaxed and let the current take her where it would.

Chapter Two

Anthony Moreno paced the aisle of the church, his thundering footsteps muffled by the thick carpet. "Somebody find her! A barefoot woman can't have gone far. Check her apartment."

People scurried to do his bidding. Anthony glanced at the red face of his father. Gemma would be punished severely for embarrassing the family this way, and it would be up to Anthony to mete out whatever punishment his father ordered.

Anthony rubbed both hands down his face. Would he have the heart to hurt Gemma? He squared his shoulders. Yes. She'd have to be taught the proper way for the wife of a Moreno to behave.

When he found out who helped her escape, he'd bury them. Anthony marched to the room where she'd have dressed and stood there, picturing her in her wedding gown, staring at the shoes left behind that had cost more than most people make in a week. He bent, grasped one, and broke off the heel before slinging it against the wall.

~

Graham O'Connor glanced twice at the woman before it registered. He hoped that second glance wouldn't cost her death. He hadn't thought twice about dropping his expensive fly-fishing rod and giving chase.

Darting along the shoreline, he searched for something to hold out as a lifeline while also doing his best to keep an eye on the woman. She'd approach a small eddy around the next bend. Hopefully, she'd be deposited there, and he could fish her out of the river.

She lay draped over a log, half in and half out of the water. Long hair the color of black coffee obscured her features.

Graham splashed into the river and gathered her in his arms. After carrying her to the bank, he laid her in the shade of an oak tree and smoothed the hair from her face. "Ma'am?" He pressed his ear to her chest. A steady heartbeat greeted him. He patted her cheek. "Miss?"

Her lashes fluttered, then eyes the same color as her hair stared up at him.

"Can you tell me your name? Is there someone I can call for you?"

"Lucy." She rolled over, coughed, and spit up enough water to make Graham raise his brows.

"Is that your name or someone I can call?" The only Lucy he knew owned the town's diner.

"My aunt." She flopped over to her back. "Thank you."

"Wow. You're Gemma Ricca." He'd seen her photo in a tabloid wrapped around a mug that the department's receptionist had given him for his birthday. What was the woman doing this far from New York?

"Please, don't tell anyone." She scooted back. "Who are you?"

"Deputy Graham O'Connor." He sat cross-legged next to her. "I really need to get you medical attention."

She shook her head. "Just take me to my aunt's."

"Does she know you're coming?"

"No." She swallowed hard and turned her face away, but not before he saw the tears.

"Okay." He'd find out why she'd come to Misty Hollow later. Graham sure hoped the Morenos wouldn't be arriving next. The sheriff wasn't going to be excited about the town's newest arrival.

He helped Gemma to her feet and, keeping one arm securely around her waist, led her to the spot where he'd left his fishing equipment. By then she seemed steady enough to walk on her own, although way too pale for his liking.

"I need my things from my car."

"Where's your car?" He lifted his tackle box and leaned his fishing pole over his shoulder.

She bit her bottom lip and furrowed her brow. "Uh…the bottom of the bottom, right where the last curve is."

"Okay. I'll take you to it." If she had a car, how did she end up in the river? Surely, she knew better than to swim in a swift current.

He stashed his equipment in his trunk and helped her into the car. "May I ask what you're doing here, Miss Ricca?"

"Call me Gemma. I'm visiting my aunt." She hiked her chin and stared out the passenger window.

Fine. Keep your secrets. He'd find out eventually. "I don't see a car." Graham parked his vehicle on the side of the road.

"It's in the water." She shoved open her door. "I swerved to miss a deer." Then she stepped to the edge of the water. "Look. I need my safe and suitcase from the trunk. I can see the taillights, so it isn't very deep." In a flash she took a step into the water.

"Hold on. You've already almost drowned once today. It's my turn." He followed her gaze. Through the murkiness of the water, he could make out the lights slowly growing dimmer. He held out his hand. "Car keys."

She cleared her throat. "They're in the ignition."

"Of course, they are." He sighed and removed his clothing, stripping down to his boxers. He handed Gemma his clothes and stepped into the water. Ice closed around his ankle. He gasped, took a deep breath, and dove in.

Using the car to pull himself along, he reached the open driver's side window and slithered in, plucking the keys from the ignition. He returned to the surface for air before diving back down. The car had sunk a few more inches. His breath wouldn't last long.

Doing his best not to float to the top, he inserted the keys into the trunk's lock. Water pressure kept the lid from propping open. He slid his fingers in and tugged upward. His lungs burned, and he kicked back to the surface.

Something pink popped up next to him, followed by a smaller silver item. He blinked the water from his lashes. A suitcase and a safe. Of course, a woman as wealthy as Gemma would have floatable possessions. He shoved them to the shore then exited the water.

"I'll have a tow truck retrieve your car as soon as possible."

"It's no good to me now." She gripped the handle of her suitcase and lifted the safe.

"We still can't leave it in the river." He took the

suitcase from her and set it inside his trunk. "This waterproof, too?"

"Yes." A slight smile graced her lips. "Not that I ever intended to find out firsthand, but it is a nice feature."

He stared at a face lovely enough to be a superstar model. "I came to catch trout and caught a socialite instead. Or are you a mermaid who's lost her fin?"

She laughed, the sound soft and husky. "I'm just Gemma Ricca."

He didn't believe that for a second.

~

How had a deputy in the middle of the Ozarks known her identity? Gemma didn't like that one bit. "I don't want anyone to know who I am."

He shot her a quick look. "Nobody in Misty Hollow will care. Who you are starts the minute you enter the town. It's a place of kind people, a welcoming spirit, and fresh starts."

Something she was hoping for. Gemma leaned her head against the seat and studied his profile. Strong, rugged. Nothing classically handsome like Anthony, but cleaner, manlier. Auburn hair struck with highlights of red, green eyes the color of spring grass, and muted freckles. This man was no king before whom people cowered. This man had honor and heart. She could tell.

"I really think you should at least let me take you to the local clinic."

"I'm fine. Thanks to you." She put a hand on his arm then pulled back as if struck. She may have come to Misty Hollow for safety, but if Anthony did find her, even suspect she'd found someone else, he'd kill him. Not even a friendship with Graham was possible. It would be best not to befriend anyone. Isolation would be the safest.

"I'm sure Lucy is at the diner. She usually is on a Saturday. If she's not expecting you, it might be a bit of a shock." Graham drove in front of a diner that looked as if it belonged in the 1950s.

"I don't know if she even knows I exist." She took a deep breath, drawing courage from the deepest part of her. "If she turns me away, I don't know what I'll do."

"Turning someone away isn't in her DNA." He tilted his head, a question in his eyes. When Gemma didn't elaborate, he shrugged and pushed his door open. "We'll go through the back. Let me have a second to prepare her. Stay in the car."

She locked the doors and slouched down the second his door closed. She'd need another pair of sunglasses, a big hat…no. She wouldn't wear a disguise. Forging a new life meant no hiding. The last place Anthony would consider looking was in the Ozark Mountains of Arkansas.

Several minutes later, Graham stepped from the building and waved her to follow. He led her around the back of the building and through a door that led into a room full of boxes and a large fridge.

A woman around Gemma's height of five-foot-nine-inches, with dyed red hair the color of another Lucy, came from the kitchen, wiping her hands on a dishtowel. She stopped a few feet away, a welcoming smile on her face. "I never thought I'd get to see you. Come here, Gemma."

"How do you know I'm who I say I am?" Tears clogged her throat.

"Because you look just like your mother, Jenny."

She held out her arms.

Gemma stepped into the warmest embrace she'd had since turning eighteen and leaving her nanny behind. "I need a place to stay."

"You've got one. A job, too, if you want."

A job sounded nice. She'd never had one.

Graham mumbled something about fetching her things and left.

Lucy held her at arm's length. "Why are you wet? Never mind. I'm taking you home, and you can tell me all about it. Chef, I'm taking a couple of hours off. I'll be back for the supper rush."

"No worries." A slightly overweight man in a stained white apron stuck his head out the kitchen door.

"Want me to put her bags in the back of your truck?" Graham waited for them behind the building.

"That would be great." Lucy patted his cheek. "You're my favorite freckle face."

His face reddened, eliciting a laugh from Gemma. "Thank you again, Graham. You saved my life." She got into a 1980-model truck while Graham put her things in the truck bed. She gave a slight wave as Lucy pulled away from the building. *Thank you* was too small for the gratitude she felt at being rescued.

Lucy's home was a small 1,000-sqare-foot ranch surrounded by acres of trees. "It ain't much, but it's home, and you're welcome to every inch of it."

"It's perfect." She smiled and retrieved her things before following her aunt to a bedroom with a queen-sized bed covered with a multi-color quilt, an armoire, and a side table. She turned to face her aunt. "Let me shower and change. Then, I'll tell you why I'm here."

"Take your time. We'll eat supper at the diner in two

hours. Will that be enough time?"

"More than enough." Gemma headed to the closet pointed out by Lucy and grabbed a towel and washcloth before entering the house's one bathroom done in gray and white.

This life was the complete opposite of the one she'd left. It would take adjustments, she might despair at times, but she could do this. Anything was better than being the wife of a Moreno. How stupid she'd been. Gemma knew enough about mobs to know that once you were in, you didn't get out except in a casket. If she'd said I do, she'd have been locked in. What an idiot not to have dug into Anthony's business a bit more. Her life of wealth and prestige had warped her thinking.

Yes, Anthony would be angry, but he'd get over her soon enough. He probably already had a new woman hanging on his arm. Why would he come for a woman who clearly didn't want him when there were plenty of others who did?

Chapter Three

Refreshed, her throat still a bit raw from the river water, Gemma joined Lucy at the kitchen table where hot cups of coffee and oatmeal cookies awaited. "Those look good."

"Graham made them." Lucy smiled. "He's always dropping off some sort of treat or another. Baking is what he does to relax after work and says he can't possibly eat it all. I know for a fact he drops off goodies at the homes of other older women. Sit and tell me your story."

"May I ask you something first?" Gemma grabbed a cookie and took a bite. Despite being soft and chewy, it stuck in her throat.

"Anything, dear."

"When my mother died, why didn't you ask for custody?" She swallowed the cookie with the help of the coffee.

"Because your father refused to allow me, a hillbilly, to have anything to do with you." She reached across the table and put her hand over Gemma's. "A hillbilly whom he could train as he did your mother was a whole other story than the sister who wanted to raise his child. No, he made me promise to stay in this hollow and leave him to raise you alone."

"I was raised by a nanny." She'd rarely seen her father until her teen years, then he'd sent her off to boarding school to learn how to act properly.

"Well, you're here now. How did you escape from your father?"

"He died three years ago of a heart attack."

"Then you are now a very wealthy young lady."

Gemma nodded. "Yesterday was my wedding day."

"Congratulations." Lucy's brow furrowed. "Shouldn't you be on your honeymoon?"

"Do you know the name Moreno?"

"Yes."

"I was going to marry Anthony Moreno. I found out shortly before the ceremony what the family business actually was. So I left." She went on to tell her aunt of her crash into the river and Graham rescuing her. "I'm never going back to New York."

Lucy sprang from her seat and wrapped Gemma in a hug. "You have a home right here with me for as long as you want one. Want a job?"

"Yes." Gemma grinned. "A new adventure."

"Do you have something a little simpler to wear?"

Gemma glanced at the linen slacks and silk, sleeveless blouse. "Jeans?" She had two pairs in her suitcase.

"And a blouse that you don't care if you stain it. We can use you at the diner, and a job will give you a purpose. No idle ladies here." Another squeeze and she stood, glancing at the clock. "Thirty minutes."

Gemma rushed back to her assigned room and put her clothes in the armoire. She eyed the engagement ring on her finger, then removed it, setting it on the polished dresser. The ring would fetch a hefty price if she ever needed the money. Or, worse case, she'd need it to barter for her freedom.

She changed into skinny jeans and studied the rest of her clothes for something simple that could be machine-washed. Yup, she definitely needed some ordinary day clothes.

Lucy knocked then entered. "Here are some shirts that should fit you until you buy your own." She laid a couple of colored tee-shirts on the bed and some cotton, flowered blouses. "You're a few inches taller than me, but they'll fit."

Gemma picked up a blouse with big pink roses on a faded cream background. "It's adorable." She slipped the blouse on and buttoned the buttons before tucking it into her jeans.

Lucy sighed. "That old blouse never looked so good. Come on. The supper rush will be starting soon, and I want to make sure to go over a few things with you. I'll have Graham take you to the mechanic tomorrow and see whether they have any cars for sale."

"I'd rather do it myself." Someone had been taking care of her for her entire life. Misty Hollow was going to be different.

"You'll need a ride there, and I won't have the time. Be independent after you purchase a car." Lucy patted her cheek. "I promise not to be a bossy aunt."

At the diner, Lucy handed Gemma a ruffled yellow apron and a pad and pencil. "Write down their orders. Drinks are free. Put the orders there." She pointed to a round thing with orders hanging from it. "When the table number is called, you pick up the order and deliver. That's it."

Sounded easy, but Gemma doubted it would be.

"This is Chef Rawlings. The other waitresses on varying schedules are Heather, Amber, and Tiffany. All are barely out of high school but are good kids and hard workers." She put her hands on Gemma's shoulders and stared into her eyes. "You got this."

Gemma bit her lip and approached a couple of men in baseball caps. "Hello, I'm Gemma. What may I bring for you?"

The men stared, then one of them laughed. "Well, listen to that fancy talk. You new to town?"

"Lucy's niece."

Loud clapping sounded from the kitchen doorway. "Folks, meet my niece, Gemma. Now, you know what that means. Respect. Ultimate respect. She's family." She pointed at the two men Gemma stood next to then went back in the kitchen.

"I can see the resemblance now," the other man said. "Except for the red hair. Welcome, Gemma. Ain't nobody going to mess you with now. That's how much we all love Lucy." They both ordered the pork chop special.

"Thank you." Gemma put the ticket where it needed to go, then turned, spotting Graham entering. She smiled and followed him to a table. "Good evening."

"Hey." His lips curved. "She has you working already?"

"It's fine, really. Do you need a minute?"

"No, I'll have the special, please." He glanced over as Lucy marched toward them.

"Tomorrow morning at nine, you will take Gemma to the mechanics to buy a car." Lucy gave a nod.

~

"I'll be working." Everyone in town was used to

Lucy's bossiness, but her niece looked taken aback.

"You know as well as I do that rarely means anything. You haven't had much to do in months. Pick her up at my house." She whipped around and strode to the kitchen.

Graham laughed. "She's right. I'll pick you up at eight-thirty. Can't let her dictate everything." His gaze fell on her left ring finger. A faint tan line showed where a ring had sat. He'd remembered seeing it on her hand yesterday. Another piece of the puzzle that was Gemma.

The next morning, Graham showed up in uniform driving a squad car. Gemma, a soft pink purse on her arm, paused on the porch before joining him. She looked classy despite the old-fashioned blouse with a frilly collar. Her dark hair had been put into some sort of twist. Simple gold earrings hung from her ears. Way too fancy of a gal for Misty Hollow. He had a feeling she could make a burlap bag look good. He opened the passenger side door. "Do you mind?"

"No, but for some reason I wasn't expecting it." She smiled. "A girl can't be any safer than with a deputy, now can she?"

"Do you need safety, Gemma?" He arched a brow hoping she'd tell him why she'd really come to Misty Hollow.

"I'm perfectly fine." Her smile slipped a little. "Let's go buy me a car."

Their eyes locked for a second, then he closed the door and loped to the driver's side. A few minutes later, he drove onto the small lot behind the mechanic's shop. A truck and two cars sat there. Nothing fancy, but they'd all get Gemma from point A to point B.

She strolled around peering in windows,

straightening when a woman pulled into the lot in a red Volkswagen convertible. "Anyone seen Joe?"

Gemma shook her head. "I'm looking to buy a car."

"Want mine? It's yours for five grand. Bought it for my granddaughter, but she wanted something else."

"Absolutely." Gemma pulled a handful of cash from her purse and counted out five thousand dollars in one-hundred-dollar bills.

The other woman's eyes widened, but she didn't hesitate to take the money. "The title's in the car. I'll get it."

"Is it bad that I kept Joe from a commission?" Gemma glanced at Graham.

"No, he won't care." He eyed her purse. "You shouldn't carry that much cash around with you."

"I'll put it in the bank. I promise." She happily accepted the key and title. "This car is adorable."

If she said so. Graham didn't think it a reasonable purchase, but it wasn't his money. "Do you know your way to the diner?"

"Yes. I'm good with directions and paid attention. Thank you."

He'd follow her back just to make sure. "Not a problem." Graham followed Gemma straight to the diner and gave a little honk as he went by. At the end of the street, he pulled into the lot across from the diner and settled in to watch for speeders. They didn't get many, but every so often, someone still tipsy from the bar at the edge of town would pass through, or a high school kid with a heavy foot would show off for the girls.

While he waited, he pulled up and read everything he could find online regarding Gemma Ricca. By lunchtime, he had a sneaking suspicion there was more to Gemma's arrival than a simple visit with her aunt. Otherwise, why the need for a job and a car? He parked and locked the car then strolled across the street to get his lunch.

Gemma laughed at something one of the diners said. Every man in the place seemed fascinated with the new gal from the big city. Graham didn't blame them. She was definitely a looker. A beautiful woman with secrets. Something this town sure didn't need.

"Good morning again." Gemma smiled, her pencil poised over her pad.

"I'll take the Reuben, thanks."

He waited until she placed his order then waved her over. "Tell Lucy you need a break. I have some questions for you."

Gemma frowned but headed to the kitchen. When she returned, she slid into the booth across from him. "I have fifteen minutes, but I'm not promising to answer your questions." She tilted her head.

"Fair enough, but one way or the other, I'll get my answers. You were supposed to marry Anthony Morena the day I fished you from the river. Did you?"

"Marry him? No." She wiggled her left hand. "I changed my mind."

"Why?" His eyes narrowed. It disappointed him that this woman he was beginning to like had ties to the mob.

She sighed. "I'd always thought the family business was in sales. I found out differently."

He gave a sarcastic chuckle. "They *are* involved in sales. Just not cars." Although, they did own a few car dealerships.

Her worried eyes met his. "I overheard Junior and Senior Moreno talking about a hit. That's when everything about them clicked into place."

"No one is that naïve." He crossed his arms. "Are you seriously telling me you didn't know they were one of the more dangerous mobs in New York?"

"I am saying that. They're careful to keep their women away from the more sordid side of things." She placed her hand on her stomach. "I'm carrying Anthony Moreno's baby."

His blood ran cold. Things were about to get very serious in Misty Hollow.

Chapter Four

Anthony clutched his cell phone so tight his knuckles ached. "Say that again."

"Miss Ricca, or is it Mrs. Moreno now? Anyway, she missed her OB appointment. She isn't answering her phone, so I'm calling to see if she wants to reschedule. She also needs to pick up her prenatal vitamins."

"Prenatal?" Gemma was pregnant?

"I'm sorry. Did you not know? I'm sure she meant to tell you in a special way." The nurse prattled on. "At twelve weeks, she wouldn't be showing yet."

Anthony collapsed into a chair. "We do plan on dinner tonight at our special place. I'll remind her then that you called. Thank you." He hung up and laid his head back, staring at the ceiling.

How dare she embarrass him by running from the altar, and now this! To take his child? He lunged to his feet. His father would know what to do.

Without waiting for an invitation, he barged into his father's office. "Gemma is pregnant."

His father steepled his fingers. "You know this how?"

"The doctor's office called. She had an appointment this morning." He sat in a leather chair across from

Anthony Senior.

"You need to find her and bring her back. Your child must be raised among his people." He picked up his phone and ordered the person on the other end to look into Gemma's family to find out where she might have gone. When he hung up, he transferred his attention back to Anthony. "We'll find her. No one stays hidden from this family for long."

"And then what? I can't force her to marry me." He plucked a piece of lint from the leg of his pants.

"Of course, you can. This explains a lot, son. Women become moody when they're pregnant. She'll come to her senses once you find her." He waved a dismissive hand. "I'm busy. Make an appointment next time you want to barge in here."

Anthony pushed to his feet and left, suddenly feeling deflated. He should've been on his honeymoon. Would Gemma have told him about the baby then? Most likely. Was the baby why she had run from their wedding? Or was it something else?

He thought back to that day she'd left and the open upstairs window. She must've heard about the hit on Esposito, something that hadn't happened yet, but Anthony was meeting with the man later that week. He frowned. The Moreno men were careful not to let the women know about the more seedy side of things, keeping them innocent and smothered in luxury. A fatal error could cost him his child.

~

Lucy stared in shock as Gemma confessed to being pregnant. One of the glasses of lemonade she held fell to the floor, spilling sweet liquid across her shoes.

Graham leaped up. "Don't move or you'll slip."

Gemma's shoulders slumped. She'd really made a mess of things. "I'm sorry, Aunt Lucy. I really am."

Her aunt tiptoed through the spilled drink as one of the waitresses grabbed a mop and bucket from the kitchen. She set the remaining glass of lemonade in front of Gemma. "It's just a surprise. Nothing we can't get through. The local clinic can take care of you and the baby until it's time to deliver."

"I had an appointment to confirm the pregnancy. Should've gone to another appointment today. I'm about three months along." She placed her hand on her stomach again. "Despite who the father is, I'm keeping my baby."

"He'll come for you." Graham returned to his seat.

"How will he know where to come?"

"It's not a secret your mother had a sister." Lucy took a fresh glass of lemonade from another server and set it in front of Graham. "He'll find me, thus finding you."

Gemma's mouth dried, and she took a huge gulp of the sugary tart drink. "He can't force me to go with him."

"Don't underestimate the Morenos," Graham said. "Lucy, if you don't mind putting this drink in a to-go cup, that would be great. I need to alert the sheriff that we might be expecting company."

Gemma needed to get back to work. If Anthony found her in Misty Hollow, he could find her anywhere. She had a new life here. If he did show up, maybe she could find a way to make him see that she wasn't part of his future. "Any more questions?" She arched a brow at Graham.

"No, you've told me plenty. Wait. Maybe one more. Does Anthony know you're pregnant?"

"I never told him."

"If he finds out, that might be the only thing that saves your life." He accepted the to-go drink from Lucy and strode to the door.

Heaving a sigh, Gemma pushed to her feet and returned to work. By the end of her shift, she barely had time to reach the bank and transfer her money. She deposited most of the cash she had, keeping a few hundred for immediate expenses, before heading back to the house she now shared with Lucy.

Since her aunt worked long hours, the house was quiet when Gemma arrived. A small package rested against the front door. Her new cell phone. A number no one else had. She called the company to set up the phone, feeling more normal than she had in a long time.

No one did for her any more. If she needed something done, she did it herself.

Grinning, she moved to the living room window that looked out onto a street with similar modest homes. A man mowed his lawn. A little boy and girl played in a sprinkler. At another house, a large Victorian slightly out of place in the neighborhood, an elderly woman pruned rose bushes. Idyllic, like a Norman Rockwell painting.

Hopefully, Anthony wouldn't arrive and ruin the peacefulness of this town. Gemma poured herself a glass of iced tea from the fridge and stepped onto the front porch. She lowered into a rocking chair and let the beauty of the town wash over her.

Folks strolled by, tossing her a wave and a hello. Most called out her name. News traveled fast, it seemed. Only a couple of days, and Gemma already felt at home.

~

Sheriff Westbrook introduced Graham to his new partner. "Meet Deputy Joey Hudson from St. Louis."

"Glad to have a partner again." Graham thrust out his hand. "We're going to need the manpower."

"Know something the rest of us don't?" The sheriff cocked his head.

"Possibly. Mind if we step into the conference room?" Graham glanced around at the people milling around the reception desk.

"Sure." Sheriff Westbrook led them down a short hall, into a room, and closed the door behind them.

Graham sat. "I'm sure you've heard of the town's new arrival."

"Lucy's niece? Yes." The sheriff and Joey sat across from him.

"She's Gemma Ricca, formerly engaged to Anthony Moreno. Fled on their wedding day. As if that isn't bad enough, she's carrying his child."

"Which means he'll be coming."

Graham nodded. "Once he finds her."

High spots of color appeared on the sheriff's cheeks. "I knew the momentary peace was too good to last. Be vigilant, guys. I'll let the others know. Graham, keep an eye on Lucy and her niece. They could be in grave danger."

"Yes, sir." Graham got to his feet. "See y'all in the morning." As he drove to the house he rented, he spotted Gemma on the front porch and stopped. "You look right at home," he said, heading up the walkway.

"This place is good for my soul. Want some tea?"

"That sounds great. Mind if I take a look around?"

Surprise registered on her face. "Sure, but why?"

"Security reasons."

She paled and nodded before entering the house.

Graham strolled to the backyard, letting himself in

through the chain-link gate. Pastureland with a few head of cattle backed up to the property. There were only a few trees, and they didn't offer much of a hiding place, although a person could easily approach the house at night.

A squirrel chattered at him from a treetop. Not much of a warning signal.

He caught sight of Gemma watching him through the kitchen window. Privileged and beautiful she was, but her life was about to implode. He didn't fault her for running. He only wished she hadn't chosen Misty Hollow. Now that she was here, he'd do everything in his power to keep her and her unborn child safe.

"What's up?" Lucy joined him. "You look like you're on official business."

"I am, sort of. I'm checking to see how safe your house is."

"My pink Glock inside says it's plenty safe."

"You might want to consider carrying it with you." He glanced at the kitchen window again. "Gemma doesn't seem overly concerned. Almost as if she's in denial about the danger. As long as she's pregnant, I don't think Moreno will harm her. *You* are a different story. As her only family member, you can be used as leverage if she resists going back to him."

"I've thought of that. Come on in. I brought home leftover lasagna for supper."

"Can't say no to that." And they could discuss safety further while eating.

Gemma handed him his tea. "I'll set another place at the table."

"My supper table has never looked this good

before." Lucy stared at the crystal goblets and nice plates. "You've raided my hutch."

Gemma gave a slight smile. "Might as well use your nice things. Graham thinks we're living on borrowed time."

"I never said that." He frowned. "However, we're dealing with some dangerous people. We can't be nonchalant."

"I'm anything but nonchalant, Deputy." She set another place setting.

"The sheriff has asked me to keep an eye on the two of you, so get used to me being here." He pulled out a chair for Gemma while Lucy cut the lasagna. "If I'd known I'd be eating here, I'd have brought a cake."

"One you bake yourself?" Lucy grinned.

"Of course." He chuckled and took his seat. "Wouldn't dare bring something store-bought."

"I'll have to taste this marvelous baking I've heard about." Gemma passed the salad bowl.

"We could have served that from the box," Lucy said. "Look at all the dishes we have to wash."

"I'll wash them." Gemma chuckled. "Live like the jewel you are."

"Honey, you might be a diamond, but I'm nothing more than a rhinestone and proud of it." She handed her a plate of lasagna, which Gemma promptly handed to Graham. Their fingers brushed, and she jerked back as if he'd stung her.

After being with Moreno, Graham couldn't fault her for being a bit gun-shy. "Thanks." As they ate, he brought up the subject of safety. "You might want to consider security cameras, an alarm…and I'll be here quite a bit."

Gemma's brows drew together. "I didn't leave one prison to be thrust into another. If Anthony does arrive, I'll simply explain to him that I no longer want to marry him. He can easily find another lady who does."

"And the baby?" Lucy asked.

Gemma released a long breath. "He is the father, but I'll find a way to prove him unfit. I will not have my child raised a Moreno."

"You're delusional." Graham shook his head. "Do you know how to shoot?"

"Never had the need to."

"You need to learn."

"Facing violence with violence is never the answer."

"This time it might be." He wasn't going to argue with her. "This is not under debate. Lucy, talk some sense into her."

"I have to agree with Graham, dear. Remember, I wasn't allowed to have anything to do with you since your birth. I was under your father's strict orders to stay away. Money and power talk. That baby will be raised Moreno. Mark my words."

"Over my dead body." Gemma crossed her arms across her belly.

That's what Graham was afraid of.

Chapter Five

Every lunchtime at the diner and every suppertime at Lucy's, Graham was there. His watchful eyes followed her every move. Was he worried she'd crack under the pressure of waiting for Anthony to arrive? What if he never came?

Gemma glowered at Graham and his partner who sat waiting for their order to be delivered. Graham's gaze softened when it met hers. He wasn't growing fond of her, was he? That wouldn't do at all. No more men or romance in her life. Just she and her baby. She had a new life and plenty of money. Soon, she'd find a house of her own. Something small and cute.

"You'll get better tips if you smile." Lucy shook her head as she passed with a tray of dirty dishes. "If you aren't feeling well, clock out."

"I'm fine." Gemma pasted on a smile and collected Graham's and Joey's order. She set their plates in front of them. "Enjoy."

"You okay?" Graham's gaze washed over her. "You seem out of sorts today."

"Hormones, I guess." She kept her smile in place and went to wait on another customer. If she kept a wall between her and Graham, he'd realize she wasn't interested, right? But what did she know about romance? There had only been Anthony since college and no one during her years in an all-girl high school. She could be imagining something that wasn't there.

Gemma froze in front of the window at the sight of a tall man with dark hair. He turned and smiled at a little boy. She relaxed. It wasn't Anthony. The man would never wear jeans and a simple tee shirt. Casual wear for Anthony was slacks and a polo shirt.

Darn Graham. His worry had her seeing danger where none existed. Maybe she could ask the sheriff to have the deputies back off. She'd been in Misty Hollow for a week with no sign of Anthony or his men.

Graham and his partner lingered in the diner until the lunch rush was over. Gemma leaned on the counter and watched as they strolled to the squad car. Graham said something that made the other man laugh.

She untied her apron and hung it on a hook in the kitchen. "I'll see you later. I have to go to my first appointment at the clinic."

"I'll be bringing home whatever we have left over after the supper crowd hits," Lucy said. "I can't wait to hear all about our little one."

Neither could she. Gemma drove her Volkswagen with the top down to the small red brick building that had once been a house but was now converted into a clinic. Next door, another former house had become a dentist office.

Dropping the keys into her purse, she entered the building and approached the reception window. "Gemma Ricca. I have an appointment."

"Oh, yes. Our latest newcomer. Welcome to Misty Hollow." The chipper woman handed her a clipboard.

"Please fill this out, and I'll need a copy of your insurance."

"I'll be paying with cash." Gemma flashed a grin and sat down to fill out the paperwork.

A few minutes later, she was waiting in a room for the doctor after being weighed. Thirty minutes later, she heard her baby's heartbeat, the doctor said she and the baby were in good health, then she paid and drove to the drugstore for prenatal vitamins. A normal, ordinary day, and she loved every minute of it.

At the house, she tossed a load of laundry into the washing machine and poured herself a glass of lemonade. She carried her drink to the front porch as she did every day after work. By now, she knew the neighbors and greeted them by name.

June Mayfield, with an oversized straw hat on her head, brought over a vase with roses from her bush. "Nothing like flowers on a dining room table to brighten up the place."

Gemma buried her nose in the blossoms. "They smell heavenly. Thank you."

"You need anything at all for yourself or the baby, you let me know. I'll find it for you." She tapped her forefinger to her temple. "Ole June has contacts."

"I bet you do." Gemma chuckled. "Again, thank you."

The old woman bustled back to her flowers. Gemma set the vase on a side table next to her rocker and picked her drink back up.

A polished Mercedes cruised down the street. The driver glanced to his left, then to his right, and back again. He slowed as he passed where Gemma sat. His eyes widened at the sight of her.

She gasped. Her glass fell to the porch, shattering into pieces. The man in the car worked for Anthony.

They'd found her.

~

Anthony patted his jacket, feeling the weight of the gun at his hip. He took a deep breath as his target exited a Jaguar. This would be his first hit. Something he knew would come someday, and something he'd dreaded.

Yes, he realized what a two-faced fool that made him, living off the money acquired from murder and other nefarious means, but he preferred paying someone else to do the dirty work. He forced a smile to his face as Esposito approached.

"Why all the secrecy? We could've met at the club, had a drink..." His eyes widened as Anthony pulled out his gun. "What is this, Junior?"

"An order from my father. Why you, Ricky? We've been friends since childhood. What has your family done?" Anthony needed to know why the hit had been placed.

The friendliness disappeared from the other man's face. "What I heard was my father undercut a business deal your father had set in place. Something I had nothing to do with. If you kill me, you'll start a war."

"Killing you makes a far better statement to your father than one of his men." Anthony shook his head. "I'm sorry." He pulled the trigger. The bullet hit his friend between the eyes.

Ricky dropped to the ground, sending up a slight cloud of dust.

With a heavy sigh, Anthony dropped a note next to the body then returned to his car. He called his father. "It's done."

"Good. Now get back here. We found Gemma."

~

Graham left the office, closing the door behind him.

"Wait up." Sheriff Westbrook hurried toward him. "Ricky Esposito has just been found dead. A note stated that Anthony Moreno took payment for Esposito Senior's betrayal."

His heart skipped a beat. "This isn't good. If Moreno comes here, Esposito won't be far behind. We'll have a gang war on our hands."

"Yep." Worry creased the sheriff's face. "Be vigilant. This little town is about to see pure evil in the hearts of men. Miss Ricca will be in the middle. Are you headed to Lucy's?"

"Yeah. I show up for supper every night, but I don't think Gemma likes it much."

"Tough. Keep it up." He clapped Graham on the shoulder. "Tell Lucy my wife sends her regards." He marched across the parking lot to his car, leaving Graham the unpleasant task of letting Gemma know what had happened.

She met him at the door. "They found me."

He didn't think it possible for his heart to stop again. At this rate, he'd have a heart attack. "Are you sure?"

"Yes." She told him of sitting on the porch and seeing the man in the car. "He definitely recognized me. Same as I did him. By now Anthony knows where I am."

He ushered her inside, locking the door. "Moreno killed Ricky Esposito this afternoon. Things are going to get ugly very quickly."

The front doorknob rattled. Graham put his hand on his weapon.

"It's Lucy." Gemma gave him a look that clearly

told him to stop overreacting. "It is her house." She peered through the peephole then opened the door. "Sorry."

"My door is never locked." She handed Gemma a bag from the diner. "Meatloaf and all the fixins. What happened?" She glanced at Graham.

He filled her in. "Time to keep that door locked at all times. Any more thought on an alarm or cameras?"

"Not necessary." Lucy led the way to the kitchen. "Anthony won't harm Gemma while she's carrying his child."

"What about you?"

She shrugged. "I'm not worried about me. Wash your hands and have a seat. Everything will be fine."

"We're going to be in the middle of a war, and this house will be ground zero."

"Fiddlesticks. Anthony will come and woo Gemma, cause some upheaval, then get bored and leave." She set the table.

"Why are the two of you so stubborn?" Seriously. They acted as if there was no danger.

"Blame it on being Italian." Gemma's laugh sounded forced. A flicker of worry crossed her eyes. "There's nothing we can do to stop this, so why work ourselves into a frenzy? We'll be safe. I promise."

There would be no such thing as safe. Graham fell into a chair. She was right, though. There'd be no stopping the coming storm. He prayed Lucy was right and Anthony wouldn't put a hit on Gemma. Once she gave birth, the danger would increase. Nothing would be able to stop Moreno from seizing his child.

The meatloaf, one of his favorites from the diner, tasted like cardboard, the mashed potatoes like paste. He eyed the living room sofa, envisioning himself sleeping there as a roadblock preventing anyone from reaching the women's rooms. Gemma would have a fit if he stayed here. She already felt imprisoned, and all he did was hang around at lunch and supper.

"You're cooking something up in that auburn head of yours." Gemma refilled his goblet of water. "You can't keep us safe, Graham. We have to do that ourselves."

"But I can try." He shoved his half-empty plate away. "It's my job."

For some reason, a look of relief crossed Gemma's face. Why would she be pleased at it being his job? He narrowed his eyes, but she looked away and mentioned to Lucy that the diner was running low on straws.

"Think of the business we'll get when the mob arrives." Lucy smirked. "There's nowhere else to eat in town. We'll be busier than ever."

"Not really. They'll refuse access to any other diners while they eat," Gemma said. "I've seen them do it before. But, you will be paid handsomely for them to do that."

Lucy's face darkened. "I won't allow that. The diners are like family. The mob will not bully me or my customers."

"You won't be able to stop them." Graham tossed his napkin on his plate. "Everything will change. You'll no longer be in control of the diner; the Morenos will. They'll dictate everyone's move."

Gemma hitched her chin. "I'll talk to Anthony. Tell him things are different here."

"I don't want you anywhere near that man!" Graham lunged to his feet.

"You have no say in what I do." Her voice rose.

"God spare me from thick-headed Italians and Irishmen." Lucy put her hands on her hips. "Why don't you go bake something and cool off, Graham. Shouting at Gemma won't make her listen to you."

"Obviously." Graham marched to the kitchen pantry and surveyed the ingredients he'd need. Lucy had everything to bake a cake. He shed his uniform shirt, draping it over a kitchen chair. It didn't matter if he got anything on the tee-shirt he wore underneath.

Gemma carried in the supper dishes and put them in the dishwasher. "You bake when you're upset?"

"Yep." Graham had a feeling there would be a lot of baking coming up. He pulled out everything he would need and set to work. Almost immediately, the stress left his shoulders. His breathing returned to normal. The heat left his face. He whistled a lively tune as he mixed the batter then poured exactly half into a pan, using the rest for another pan.

He peered up. Gemma stood immobile at the sink, staring out the window.

Not bothering to wipe his hands, he joined her. A man in a dark suit stood on the other side of the chain-link fence. Not Moreno. Graham would recognize him from his photos. No, this was a hired hand keeping an eye on the prize.

Chapter Six

A knock sounded at the front door. Graham shook his head when Gemma started to answer. "I'll get it."

Her heart beat in her throat. She didn't need to see who stood on the porch. It would be Anthony. The man behind the house never went anywhere without his boss.

Graham opened the door a few inches. "Can I help you?"

"I'm here for Gemma Ricca, my fiancée." Anthony's smooth, cultured voice reached her ears. "It's time for her to come home."

"Pretty sure this is her home now." Graham shot her a look.

"I'd like to speak with her, please."

Gemma stepped between the two men. "We can talk on the porch." She gripped the doorknob. "We'll be fine, Deputy." It was best if Anthony knew right off that Graham was not anything more than local law enforcement. Her gaze locked with Graham's as she pulled the door closed behind her. "Have a seat, Anthony."

"Don't I deserve a kiss?" He leaned in, frowning when she offered her cheek. "What is this, Gemma?"

"Please sit." She lowered into a rocking chair well aware that every eye on the street was looking their way.

A muscle ticked in his clean-shaven jaw. A hardness settled over his features. "Why did you run? I can give you everything you've ever dreamed of."

"I have money of my own, Anthony." She took a deep breath. "I cannot be a part of your family business. What you sell isn't what I thought. There are other women who will be more than happy to be your wife."

"You're carrying my child." His voice became a growl. "You will not take my child away. I see from your expression you didn't expect me to find out. Guess you shouldn't have put me down as your contact number at the doctor's office."

He was right. How could she have been so stupid? The nurse had gushed over the fact that Gemma and Anthony were getting married. Of course, they'd call him.

"I cannot have my child raised believing that killing, trafficking, and stealing are normal facts of life." She gripped the arms of the rocking chair. Her fingernails dug into the wood. A neighbor called out a greeting, and she pasted on a smile.

"This small-town life doesn't suit a woman like you." He gripped her arm hard enough to leave bruises. "You can't fight me on this. Gemma, you loved me once. It will all come back to you, I promise. This is nothing more than hormones."

Oh, please. "You're hurting me."

"My apologies." He released her. "I'm not quite sure where to go. There's no hotel suitable in this…place."

"You can't stay here."

He arched a brow. "Why? Will the deputy mind?"

"He's a friend of my aunt's, nothing more."

"Imagine my surprise when I found out you had family alive." His tone made his words sound like a threat.

"Leave her alone." Gemma pushed to her feet. "Find someone else, Anthony."

"No other woman is carrying my child." He stood and marched toward the black Jaguar parked in front of the house. "I'll speak with you further on this matter at a later time."

Rather than watch him leave, she went back into the house and into her aunt's arms.

"Come on. Graham, I think the cake is ready. Chocolate cake is the perfect pick-me-up." Lucy led Gemma to the kitchen.

"How did I get into this mess?" She sat and covered her face with her hands. "He'll never let me be."

"Probably not." Lucy rubbed her back. "You fell in love and got pregnant. Sweetie, you aren't the first, and you won't be the last. You just chose the wrong man."

Graham set a slice of cake in front of her.

"Thanks," she mumbled. "I need to find a way to make him move on." She glanced at Graham. "Can't you find enough dirt on him to lock him up?"

A dimple winked in his cheek. "I'll be trying to help NYPD prove he killed Esposito. Anything else I find will be icing on the cake. We'll have him behind bars before your baby is born."

She really hoped so. Gemma wanted to believe in Graham's confidence, but Anthony Senior had managed to escape prison, and the man was approaching sixty. She picked up her fork and dug into the cake. "You should be a private chef." Her eyes lit up. "This is the best cake I've ever tasted."

"Can't cook, only bake." He grinned and sat across from her. "Chin up, Gemma. Lucy and I will help you through this. Heck, the whole town will. You became one of us the second Lucy introduced you."

She wanted him to promise, although she knew it wasn't a promise he could keep. Gemma nodded and continued eating. He made everything sound possible, but then Graham had never lived under the same roof as a Moreno. The family had only one agenda . . . to get what they wanted.

~

The next morning, Anthony drove back to Misty Hollow, having barely slept in the three-star motel in Langley. Where was the culture, the luxury? Fine dining didn't exist. He'd passed a diner on his way to see Gemma. Hopefully, the coffee wouldn't be horrible.

"Turn in here, Robert," he told his driver. "Wait in the car. I'll have something sent out to you. I don't want to attract too much attention."

Something he didn't accomplish. Every head in the place swiveled to stare as he entered. The deputy from Gemma's aunt's house and another one fixed hard stares on him.

"Only one?" A pretty young girl grabbed a menu. When Anthony nodded, she led him to a table near the window. "Your server will be with you shortly."

He sneered and perused a menu of greasy food and omelets. He'd die of clogged arteries before Gemma came to her senses. Unless . . . He glanced out the window. This town might be the perfect place to build his own empire.

The scenery couldn't be beat outside of an ocean view. He'd purchase a large chunk of land and build a resort that included everything this town and the surrounding cities lacked. Anthony smiled and glanced up as footsteps approached. His smile faded at seeing Gemma in a ridiculous yellow apron.

"You work here?" His eyes widened.

"Yes." A slight smile tugged at her lips. "I'm enjoying being ordinary."

"You could never be ordinary. Don't be ridiculous. You'll tire of whatever game you're playing soon enough. Just get it out of your system before our baby is born." He handed her the menu. "Two coffees, black, and two meat-lover omelets. Take one order to Robert outside."

A stubborn look crossed her face. "Say, please."

"What?" He frowned.

"Say, please. I'm not someone you can boss around any longer." She tilted her chin.

Who was this woman? "Please."

"Thank you. I'll have your order right out." Back straight, she turned in his order, then approached the deputies, refilling their coffee mugs.

Anthony waved her over. "You need to quit working here. It isn't good for the baby."

Her brow furrowed, something he hated. She'd wrinkle. "Waiting tables will not hurt the baby, and it gives me something to do. As I said, I'm not someone you can order around."

She hadn't been lying when she'd said she had her own money. Gemma's parents had left her very well off, so why the menial labor? Had the pregnancy affected her brain?

After she turned to wait on someone else, he sent a text to the office in New York to begin a search for land for sale around Misty Hollow. If Gemma wanted to stay here, then he'd build her a palace.

~

"That man is going to be everywhere Gemma is," Graham said, staring into his coffee.

"The worst possible shadow." Joey glared at the mobster. "Any luck on getting the proof you're looking for?"

"Not yet. No one saw anything. The shooting took place in a vacant field. All I've got are tire tracks. Moreno isn't the only person in New York to drive a Jaguar. Besides, I've been told it's out of my jurisdiction and to let NYPD handle the murder."

"Tough break." Joey continued to watch Moreno. "He'll do something here that we can nail him on."

"Hopefully, someone won't have to die for us to get that something."

Gemma set a plate in front of the man, poured his coffee, then carried a to-go box and cup outside.

Graham leaned forward to get a better view. "Sidekick stayed in the vehicle. I wonder what Moreno is planning."

"What do you mean?" Joey followed his gaze.

"He doesn't strike me as a man who would simply follow a woman around. He'd pay someone to do that. What does he have up his sleeve?"

"Whatever it is won't be good." Joey finished his coffee and stood. "Ready? The sheriff wants us to check out the high school football field. Said some kids have been painting on the underside of the bleachers."

It beat sitting around wondering what Moreno was

up to. Gemma was safe enough at the diner. Every person in the place would come to her aid if she needed them. He tossed enough money on the table to pay for their meals and a tip.

Gemma smiled as they passed. "See you later."

Graham couldn't resist shooting Moreno a glance. If looks could kill, he'd be dead. Chuckling, he followed Joey from the diner.

Since it was early afternoon, students were absent from the field, holed up in classrooms while teachers did their best to teach. Graham and his partner ducked under the bleachers. Gum and a lewd drawing of a particular part of the male anatomy decorated the bottom of the seats.

"Isn't this something the maintenance crew should take care of?" Joey posted his hands on his hips and stared at the painting.

"I think the sheriff wants us to put the fear of God in some high school kids." Graham shook his head and laughed. "Wants us to show up at the pep rally and make a little speech."

"It won't work. The kids will just get sneakier and more creative."

"Vandalizing the bleachers with nasty artwork is better than drugs, in my book." But, the sheriff had said to give the speech, so he would. In his day, they'd had street rod races and spun doughnuts in the practice field after a heavy rain. Law enforcement had run off Graham and his buddies plenty of times. He glanced at his watch. "About time for that speech."

"I haven't been to a pep rally since I graduated." Joey grinned. "Might be fun. Let's save the speech until the end."

This was what law enforcement in Misty Hollow was supposed to be like. Easy days, with little to no danger. Friendly folks who waved and called out greetings as they drove past. They might as well enjoy it while they could.

The arrival of Anthony Moreno would change all that. He might be on his best behavior at the moment, but the man was dirty. He could only act clean for so long. When he let go of the façade, Graham would be there to nab him.

Chapter Seven

A week later, Anthony strode into Ray's, a local bar, and surveyed the scene. In his hand, he carried rolled blueprints. Motorcycles lined the space in front of the rough, wood-hewn building. Research had shown that the bar changed hands more than a poker player.

His lip curled. The place smelled of sweat, beer, and a tinge of vomit. Did these people have no pride? Anyway, the place was his now. He had plans on a complete renovation that did not include bikers.

Snapping his fingers, he motioned for the hired hands to clear the place out. Curses and fist fights broke out until Anthony pulled his gun from his boot and fired a round into the ceiling. "I own this place now, gentlemen. We're going to upscale a bit. Check in with us in a few weeks." Not that any of them had a chance of gaining entry into what would be his classy nightclub, Gemma's. That ought to be a step to making her happy. The only place in this hick town suitable for her would have her name lit up in neon.

He sat at a table and ordered a whiskey from the shocked bartender. The man wasn't too rough in appearance. If he cleaned up nice, he'd stay on. Anthony eyed the few women servers. Only one would look good in the uniform she'd have to wear. He waved for Robert to come over.

"Keep the young brunette. Get rid of the others. Send the brunette to me."

"Yes, sir." Robert left to do his bidding.

While Anthony waited, he unrolled the blueprint. He'd had it drawn up without seeing the place first, but the plan ought to work well enough. The arrival of the construction crew drew his attention seconds before the drink server stood in front of him.

"Sit down. I'll be right back." Anthony went to greet the crew. "Do the manager's office first. I need a place to work. I expect it to be done by eight a.m. I'm paying you to be quick." The club should be up and running by week's end. Money could get anything done quickly.

Maybe he'd make Gemma happy and build a life here, change the town to something to be proud of. It was worth a thought. He returned to the table.

"How old are you?"

"Twenty-two." Heavily made-up brows drew together.

"You always wear that much makeup?"

"Yeah."

"It's yes, sir." He crossed his arms. "If I'm to keep you, the makeup would have to be toned down. I'll have someone help you. How much do you make?"

"Minimum wage."

"I'll pay you twenty dollars an hour. You'll wear this." He showed her a picture of a woman in a bustier, thong, fishnet stockings, and boots that went above the knee. "No one will be allowed to lay a hand on you, but a pretty girl wearing very little clothing brings in the drinkers. Do you have any lovely friends who would be interested? The bar will open every evening at eight and close at two a.m."

She gave a slow nod, her gaze wary. "You aren't going to sell our, uh . . . . "

"Not unless you want to." He arched a brow. "I already have girls for that, but—"

"Oh, no, sir, but I will serve the drinks."

"Good. You're off until we open one week from today. Pick up your uniform the day before. You'll sign a contract saying you agree to wear the lingerie, and that you will not gain more than ten pounds while employed here. I'll have the papers ready when you pick up your uniform. Call your friends. I need to know now." He waved her away. "Go over there until you're finished."

She pulled a cell phone from the tight jeans she wore and started making calls as she moved to the opposite side of the room.

Anthony unrolled the blueprint that was his favorite. A casino resort. The top floor would be his and Gemma's penthouse home. The whole thing would be built on the mountaintop overlooking a lake and would be complete by the time his child was born.

~

Gemma overfilled the cup of the big man in a leather vest sitting in the booth. "The new bar is named what?"

"Gemma. Same as your name tag. Hey—" His eyes narrowed. "Is the bar named after you?"

Unfortunately, that was most likely the truth. "I'm sure it's a coincidence, but it's a real shame that a landmark such as that place is being changed." She had no idea if the bar was a local landmark or not, but it eased some of the anger on the man's face. Sorrow replaced the anger.

"Yeah, it is. Heard it's going to be some posh nightclub with naked girls. You know how word spreads in this town."

Her hand shook as she wiped up the spilled coffee. "When will it be finished?"

"In a week. Can you believe that? I heard a man can't even get in unless he's wearing a suit. Gals got to dress up too. Going to be a real swanky place." He tugged on the ragged beard on his face. "Maybe I can get in if I trim this up. Since I'm a lawyer, I have plenty of suits."

Gemma laughed. "You don't look like a lawyer."

"What's a lawyer look like?" He grinned. "I'm not one of those from New York."

She patted his shoulder. "No, sir, you aren't." She'd never met anyone like the people of this town and loved every one of them.

Graham and Joey entered and headed to their same booth that faced the door and the windows. The only thing that changed was who had the better view of the window that day. She grabbed two mugs and carried them to their table. "Guess you heard about the nightclub?"

Graham nodded. "As soon as the contract was signed." His worried gaze studied her face. "How do you feel about the name?"

"I hate it. It's a ploy that won't work." She shuddered. "He'll destroy my reputation."

"Nothing can do that. You're one of us." He smiled. "I'll have the day's special."

"I'll have the same," Joey said.

"You don't even know what it is." She laughed.

"Doesn't matter. Everything Chef Rawlings cooks

is great."

Her smile faded. "This is going to increase crime, isn't it?"

"Absolutely. Moreno will bring in drugs and prostitution. It's going to be a full-time job to stop him."

Gemma had to figure out a way to stop Moreno before what made this town special disappeared. She took their orders to the chef's window and refilled the pot of coffee. Her face heated as Moreno strolled in as if he owned the place.

His gaze swept the room, falling on her. He moved her way. "Time for you to quit this place, Gemma. I've something else for you to do."

"Manage your strip club?" She set the pot down and crossed her arms. "I won't do it."

"I need someone to keep the girls in line. With your class and poise, you're perfect." He set his jaw. "I'm doing this for you."

"Stop. I don't want any of it. I've already told you I enjoy working here. So stop it." She snatched the pot from the counter and went to refill cups, but he was right behind her.

"I won't chase you for long." Anthony's breath tickled the hairs on the back of her neck. "Remember that." He planted a soft kiss on her neck then sauntered from the diner.

Her skin crawled, and she wanted to scrub the back of her neck with steel wool.

"That man bothering you?" The bearded lawyer asked. "'Cause after him running us out of our hangout, me and the boys would like nothing better than to put him in his place." He pounded a fist into his palm.

"It's fine, but thank you for the gesture." Lord, all

she needed was for the bikers to start a war with the Morenos. She went to fetch his burger, wrapped in a warm hug by the man's concern.

This was all her fault. Maybe no one could win against the Morenos. She should have stayed in New York and spared this lovely town. How could she get through to Anthony?

Tears pricked her eyes. Seemed she was growing more emotional every day. She rushed to the restroom to rinse her face, thankful she hadn't experienced morning sickness. Gemma put a hand under her apron and over the slight mound of her stomach. She would never be able to keep this child from growing up under Anthony's thumb which started the tears up again.

Enough. Gemma washed her face again and returned to her job. She'd think of something. She had to.

~

Later that afternoon, Graham tagged along as Sheriff Westbrook visited the nightclub. Workers buzzed around the inside and outside like carpenter ants. Already, aluminum replaced the wooden siding. A crane was lifting a giant neon sign with *Gemma* in big letters next to a martini glass. Things were moving way faster than he liked.

The sheriff shook his head and pushed open the double doors then stared at the black paint on his hand. "A sign would've been helpful."

Graham lifted his palm. "I'm not touching anything but metal surfaces." He grabbed a rag from the bar counter when they entered and handed it to the sheriff.

"Thanks." He wiped his hand as his eyes swept the room. "There."

Moreno exited the men's room. Spotting them, he approached with a smile. "Welcome. I do hope the two of you will be frequent guests." He held his hand to the sheriff who ignored the gesture.

"Do you have a place where we can talk?"

"My office isn't quite finished, so we'll sit at a table. Can I get you gentlemen a drink?"

"This isn't a pleasure call." Graham sat. "Mr. Moreno, we're aware that several of your clubs have been involved in drug trafficking and prostitution. I want to make you aware that this will not be tolerated in Misty Hollow. You won't be able to bribe us to look the other way." The sheriff's features hardened.

"I assure you that everything will be aboveboard." Moreno steepled his fingers and peered at Sheriff Westbrook. "You should know very well how we work, having married Bartelloni's daughter. Why, I even heard you worked for her father for a while."

"As part of a case. We aren't here to talk about me or my wife, Mr. Moreno." He pushed to his feet. "I fully expect you to understand that the law will be strictly enforced in my town."

"I'm fully aware." Humor sparked in the other man's eyes. "Come visit on your day off. You might enjoy yourself. I'm sure the two of you can see your way out."

Outside, Graham rolled his shoulders. "I feel like I need a shower after talking to that man."

"That's the evil that pours off of him." He stared at Graham over the top of the car. "I'm sure you knew I'm former FBI and worked undercover as a bodyguard for Bartelloni."

"No, but it doesn't matter to me. What matters is

now." And keeping Gemma out of the mobster's hands.

"This is bad." Sheriff Westbrook took a deep breath. "Maybe the worst yet since I've been sheriff."

"We'll get through this." He clapped him on the shoulder. "Johnson and Young are great deputies. Joey is coming along great. We can always ask for help, temporarily deputize some men."

"I've had to do that before." He opened the door and slid into the driver's seat. "There's a few men in this town up for the task. You still keeping an eye on Ms. Ricca?"

"As often as I can. It gets to her at times. Reminds her too much of being with Moreno and his goons."

"I don't care. Once that baby is born, if she hasn't gone to him, she won't be safe."

Graham agreed, and the thought terrified him. His heart raced, and his palms sweated. He could not let Moreno draw her back into his lifestyle or harm her in any way.

Chapter Eight

Gemma stepped outside the next morning to the sight of the largest vase of red roses she'd ever seen. Lying next to them was a white jeweler's box. With a huff she glanced at the man sitting in the Jaguar. "Return these to your boss, Robert." She strode to her car and climbed into the driver's seat.

And now it started. He'd ply her with gifts the same as he'd done when they started dating. It had worked to lure her in then; it would not work now.

Robert left his car and hurried across the lawn toward the porch, then he approached her car. "Can't you just accept them? You don't have to like the gifts. Gemma, you know how he'll react when I take these back."

"Give them to your wife."

He paled. "He'd kill me."

She shrugged. "That's the life you chose. I don't want them." She turned the key in the ignition and backed from the drive. Her knuckles whitened from her grip on the steering wheel as all the worries from the day before fell on her shoulders.

With a sigh, she felt her stomach. "Well, little bambino, things are not going to be easy, are they?" She smiled and waved as she drove down Main Street. The idyllic peacefulness of the town was going to be shattered now that Anthony had arrived. The "businesses" he'd bring weren't family-friendly or safe.

She parked alongside the diner, leaving the front spots open for customers. As soon as she entered the building, the sheriff waved her to a table where he sat with a pretty red-haired woman.

"Gemma Ricca, meet my wife, Karlie Westbrook." The soft gaze he gave his wife melted Gemma's heart. Would a man ever look at her that way? "Lucy said we could speak with you before you start your shift."

She glanced at the clock. Thirty minutes before the rush. "Okay." Puzzled, she sat across from them.

Karlie held out her hand. "Glad to meet you. Welcome to Misty Hollow."

"Thank you." Gemma liked the woman immediately. "What do you want to talk to me about?"

"Anthony Moreno." The sheriff folded his hands on the table.

She didn't anticipate liking what he was going to say. Her brow arched, but she said nothing.

"Graham has told us that you are avoiding Moreno, that you want him to go away and leave you alone." He raised his hand as she started to speak. "I don't blame you, but this is my town. I need him put away so he doesn't come back. People will die with him around."

Karlie reached across the table and took Gemma's hand. "My father is Anthony Bartelloni."

Gemma ran the name through her mind before recognizing the man. "Wow. Looks like Anthony is a popular name for Italians."

Nodding, she chuckled and continued. "So, I

understand where you're coming from, I truly do. You see, I had to agree to get to know my father in order to put him behind bars."

Throat threatening to close, Gemma forced out, "You want me to spy on Anthony?"

The other woman gave a sheepish smile. "Sort of, yes. We want you to go along with what he wants. If you're under his roof, you'll be able to hear and see things. It won't take long for him to trust you again."

"He never told me anything before this." It would never work.

"But now, you know." She tilted her head. "Are you sure he'll keep you safe once your baby is born?"

Gemma placed her hands over her stomach. "No." In fact, Anthony would probably get rid of her so he could raise the baby in the way he wanted. Maybe their idea had merit after all. She'd lived with him before. Could she again? Could she blame her behavior and emotions on being pregnant? She glanced from Karlie to the sheriff. "How would I communicate with you? After I ran off, Anthony would keep me under lock and key. I'd have a chaperone."

"We've got a man on the inside. FBI. I can't tell you more than that."

"So, you've been thinking about this for a while?"

He nodded. "Since Moreno showed up in our town."

Anthony wouldn't allow her to work at the job she liked. There's be no sitting on the front porch waving at the neighbors. Everything she'd come to love would be gone. She truly didn't want to go to New York. Hopefully, Anthony wanted to stay here. If she had to go back to him, she'd rather it be here than there. But if she went back to him, it would keep the people she cared about safe.

"Okay, I'll do it. But once my baby is born, if Anthony isn't in prison, I'll disappear." If he didn't snatch her child upon birth. The very thought made her heart seize. She should've fled the moment he arrived in town.

~

Anthony stood on the edge of the mountain and smiled at the view of the town and lake below him. "This is the perfect spot for my resort." He glanced at the realtor, a pretty blonde in a red suit. "Make it happen."

"Yes, sir." She grinned, obviously aware that her commission would be a nice chunk of change. "I'll bring the paperwork to your place tonight?" She bit her bottom lip.

Why not? "Sure. Plan on staying a while." A man had needs after all, and he'd left his mistress in New York. Why not have one here, too? "I want to break ground in the morning."

Shock crossed her features. "It'll take time—"

"This will be my land. Contact the owner and ask them how much they want to let me get started before my name is on the title." Why did people make things harder than they needed to be? Anthony had to prepare Gemma's home for her. He couldn't have his child growing up in the old Victorian he rented while waiting for the resort.

He'd have to do some renovations on the house in case things ran late. The work piled up. Did he want to stay in this town? Building meant putting down roots. Everything in New York belonged to his father. Yes, he would build his empire here.

~

"You did what?" Graham shot to his feet. "Why would you put her back under his thumb?"

"We need proof he killed Esposito to pass on to NYPD. And we need to know what he has planned for Misty Hollow." The sheriff wouldn't be deterred.

"Gemma isn't law enforcement." He ran his hand roughly through his hair, wincing as his fingers caught in a tangle. "What if she's not a good actress?"

"She will be. Gemma will do anything to protect her child."

"You're a husband and father." Graham shook his head. "I can't see how you'd allow this. What if it was your wife?"

"It once was. We accomplished what we wanted to."

"This isn't the same. Bartelloni wouldn't kill his daughter."

"No, but he might kill her mother. It's already done, Graham. She'll be approaching him later today."

Not if he had anything to do about it. Graham whipped around and stormed out of the building and to the diner. He could have driven the couple of blocks but wanted to burn off steam before confronting Gemma.

She was refilling a man's coffee cup when he arrived at the diner and stopped her before she entered the kitchen. He took the pot from her hands and pulled her into a corner booth. "What were you thinking?" He kept his voice low, but the words still sounded like a growl.

"That I can be beneficial in putting Anthony behind bars."

"Don't do this. It's too dangerous." He took her hands in his.

"I've already said I would." She pulled free. "He'll

go after my aunt in order to get to me if I don't. I'm surprised he hasn't already threatened her. Lucy is all I have left, Graham. This is something I can do."

"Can you?" He narrowed his eyes. "Can you let him kiss you? Can you sleep by his side? Can you pretend to like his affection without cringing? Because if you can't, he'll make you regret it."

"You act as if you know him." She paled.

"All I do in my spare time is read everything I can find about the Moreno family. Maybe Anthony won't hurt you, but his father is another story." He wanted her more frightened than she'd ever been in her life so she'd come to her senses.

"I appreciate your concern, but you really have no say in what I do." Resolution settled across her face.

Her words stung. He wanted the right to express his feelings, tell her how much she'd come to mean to him, but he couldn't. Graham had thought she might start to feel the same for him. Her cold words and tone spoke clearly about her feelings.

He stood. "Sorry to have bothered you." Back straight, he strode out and headed to the office.

Joey pulled the squad car up to the curb. "Hop in. We're supposed to go take a look at the progress on Moreno's nightclub. You okay?"

"Yeah." He slid in the passenger side. "The sheriff has convinced Gemma to go back to Moreno and spy."

His eyebrows raised. "Risky."

"Yeah." He blew his breath out in a steady stream. "Looks like I'm not needed to keep an eye on her anymore."

"At least not at her house." He shot Graham a sympathetic look. "It's never wise to fall for an assignment."

"I'm only concerned." Liar. He remained silent the rest of the way. When they arrived at the bar, the new neon sign had been installed. At least it wasn't flashing Gemma's name yet. He shoved his door open with more force than necessary and slid out.

New dark aluminum siding covered the once-rough walls and windows. New double doors to match the siding had replaced the old metal ones.

"Looks like Moreno doesn't want anyone being able to look in from the outside," Joey said.

As they approached the door, a large man with biceps the side of Graham's head greeted them. He held a clicker in his hand and pressed it twice.

"Letting Moreno know how many law enforcement showed up?" Graham tilted his head.

The man said nothing but pressed the earpiece he wore, listened, then stepped aside to hold the door open. "Go on."

The place had changed virtually overnight. A new mirror hung behind the bar with glass shelves displaying liquor bottles in an array of colors. Padded stools with backs lined the bar. Glass tables and black leather chairs filled the room. On the opposite end stood a platform with a stripper pole. Real classy. Graham rolled his eyes.

Across the building, he led Joey to a door almost hidden behind a post. If Moreno wanted to be close but not easily found, this is where he'd want his office. Next to it sat the room where the previous owner had been murdered a while back.

He rapped twice and exchanged a wary glance with Joey. A few seconds later, they were told to come in.

Moreno sat behind a polished walnut desk. "What

can I do for our local law enforcement officers?"

"We're here to see the progress, nothing more. Mind if we take a look around, or would you rather give us a tour?"

"Not too much to see other than the girls' changing room and the kitchen." He pushed to his feet. "But, I'm a nice guy, so I'll give you the tour myself. The two of you might as well be the first to know . . . I've purchased quite a few acres on top of the mountain for my Paradise in Misty Hollow Resort. Maybe I should take you there next?" He arched a brow.

Graham's heart sank. With the amount of money he threw around, this man had no intentions of going anywhere.

Chapter Nine

Gemma dressed in the nicest thing she owned that still fit. A flowing summer dress the color of the sky on a clear day. The dress had always made her feel pretty. She put her hair in a French twist, applied minimal makeup, and mentally prepared herself to speak with Anthony. It would have to happen most likely at the nightclub. She shuddered thinking of the place.

Gemma drove her little car to the nightclub. The men guarding the door barely spared her a glance as she waltzed inside. After all, the place bore her name. She had a right to be there.

The bartender motioned his shining bald head toward an unmarked door. Keeping her features neutral, Gemma entered without knocking.

A blond woman in a royal-blue suit hopped off the corner of Anthony's desk. He simply gave a saccharine smile and waved the woman away. "Gemma."

"Anthony." Gemma stared after the fleeing woman then closed the door. "Didn't take you long to choose your latest." She sat, arranging the hem of her dress to cover her legs.

He steepled his fingers, a younger version of his father. "Have you decided to come back to me?" He pulled the white box that had been on her porch from a desk drawer and slid it across the desk. "You rejected my gift."

"As a matter of fact, I have. But—" She raised a brow. "I will continue working at the diner until I'm close to giving birth. My aunt needs me, and I have friends there. You will not treat me as a possession any longer. I will have freedom, Anthony, or I walk, and you never see me or this child again."

His eyes flashed. "You could never go far enough that I couldn't find you, but I'll indulge your silly whim. Work as a peasant if it makes you happy. Now, open the gift and put it on."

"And if I don't, what then?"

"Don't make me angry, Gemma. I'm willing to compromise with you." He pushed the box closer.

She snatched it from the desktop and opened it to reveal a diamond tennis bracelet. "It's lovely."

"It was meant to be worn at our wedding." He rose from his chair and came to her side. "Let me clasp it on your wrist."

Gemma fought not to shudder at his touch, at the hands that had killed. She studied the bracelet closely once it was on. The overhead light shot prisms of light through the stones. She sighed, knowing it most likely held a tracker.

He held out his hand. "I have something else to show you. Will you come?"

She stared at his hand for a moment then nodded. Slipping her hand in his, she stood. "I'm off today, so I have plenty of time."

"Not as much as you'd think. You need to gather your things. First, I'll show you your new home then the big surprise."

"This place isn't the surprise?"

He shook his head. "I'd like you to come to the Grand Opening tonight and look over the girls I've hired. They'll need a lady to help keep them from acting like country bumpkins."

Gemma rolled her eyes, fully aware of the kind of girls she'd be looking over. She meekly followed him to his car not wanting to disturb the uneasy truce by dragging her feet.

He drove to a large Victorian one block from where she lived with her aunt.

"It's gorgeous."

"Wait until you see the inside." He grinned and went to open her door for her.

"You've renovated a rental?"

"The old biddy who owned this place refused to allow me to do anything, so I purchased it. Then I had to pay off the historical society. You'll see that it's all worth it. Besides, it's only until my surprise is complete." He unlocked the front door and pushed it all the way open.

A sweeping staircase, thankfully still with its original wood, led to the second floor. Modern marble covered the floors. A peek through the door to her right showed a fireplace covered in marble. Gemma bet it had once been stone.

"Well?"

"It's lovely, but such a pity to get rid of so many historical elements."

Anthony's smile faded. He shook his head. "Modern is the way to go. Imagine how much we can sell this house for when we no longer need it. Come. I'll show you your room. Feel free to decorate it any way you choose."

Her room contained a king-sized, four-poster bed, an antique armoire, a stone fireplace, and a rocking chair. A handmade quilt covered the bed. Sheer curtains were tied back to the posts. The same sheers covered the bedroom window. "I won't change a thing."

"You might feel differently about the bathroom." He led her to a room with a pink tub, toilet, and sink.

She laughed. "Okay, this one we'll change."

"It's good to see you laugh again."

She fought to keep the smile on her face. "What's this big surprise?"

"I'll be happy to show you." He drove her to an expanse of land on top of the mountain. A large pile of downed trees sat off to one side. "Don't worry. They won't go to waste. We'll use as much of the local material as possible for Paradise in Misty Hollow."

She shot him a questioning look.

"A resort, darling, with a penthouse for us and our child on the top floor. This is all ours." He climbed from the car. After helping her out, he led her to a cliff edge. "Look at that view. People will pay money to come here. We'll have a spa, casino—"

"Gambling is illegal here."

His laugh boomed over the valley. "Money takes care of things like that, my dear. You should know that by now. Money takes care of everything."

Not everything.

~

"Why me and Joey?" Graham couldn't believe they'd been hired to attend the Grand Opening of Gemma's.

"I want eyes in the place—tonight especially." Sheriff Westbrook slipped his handgun into its holster. "I don't want to go alone. Johnson and Young will take any calls that come through while we're out."

"In addition to keeping order, you want us to watch for anything illegal or stay as inconspicuous as possible?"

"Inconspicuous."

Graham agreed. "So, plain clothes." Being out of uniform would make the others in attendance more comfortable.

"Suits." Westbrook flashed a grin. "Hope you have one."

"I do." Although he preferred jeans and tee-shirts. A button up on special occasions.

"See you outside the nightclub at eight." Westbrook hurried from the office, leaving Graham to make his way home.

He pulled his suit from the closet and unzipped the garment bag. He hadn't worn the suit since his father's funeral three years ago. It would be out of date to Moreno's standards. Still, if the club's dress code required a suit, he'd be wearing one.

At precisely five minutes 'til eight, He entered the club's parking lot, surprised at the number of vehicles. Graham hadn't thought the people of Misty Hollow would welcome such a place. A few license plates from neighboring states partially explained the number of vehicles.

The sheriff and Joey met him as he crossed the parking lot and got in line. "You clean up good, O'Connor."

"We Irish are great actors." Graham made a big deal

of straightening his tie.

All laughter vanished when he entered and saw Gemma, hair up, wearing a burgundy night dress cut up to the thigh on one side. A high neckline and a plunging back where fabric pooled at her waist. A diamond bracelet sparkled like the earrings on her ears. His mouth dried up at the sight of her.

Her smile looked forced as she greeted them. "Welcome to Gemma's, Gentlemen. Drinks are on the house tonight."

A woman wearing lingerie led them to a table. The sheriff shook his head and moved to a table that allowed a view of the door. She shrugged and sashayed away.

Loud music started a few minutes past eight, and a woman only wearing a thong danced around the pole on the platform in the center of the room. Graham averted his gaze and held up his hand. He considered the night a working one and ordered a sparkling water.

"That's all?" The server tilted her head.

"Make that three," the sheriff said.

The woman frowned and shrugged. "You must be cops." She headed for the bar, returning later with their drinks.

Graham was pretty sure this would be the last time she'd approach their table. He sighed and searched the room for Gemma.

She sat at a table in the corner, alone, looking more beautiful than any woman had the right to. He'd thought her pretty before, but man . . . .

"She's too classy for this town." Joey clapped his shoulder. "Best put your eyes back in your head and find a girl more suited to an Irish deputy."

Graham slapped his hand away. "Like you have any

room to talk. Where's your girl?"

"Haven't found her yet." He raised his glass in a toast. "Here's to Sheriff Westbrook, the only one who's found his girl."

"Here, here." Graham clicked his glass against theirs. Wrong, he'd found *his* girl. The problem was she was out of his reach.

Gemma stood and stepped in front of one of the working girls leading a man to a back room. She shook her head and pointed for them to return to the bar area, her eyes flitting to where Graham and the others sat. Guilt marred her pretty features.

"That's a mite suspicious," Joey said. "Think there's going to be prostitution here?"

"I'm guessing there might be but not tonight," the sheriff answered. "Not while we're here."

"I still plan on eating lunch at the diner every day. I'll ask Gemma tomorrow." Graham wouldn't let a day go by without laying eyes on her and knowing she was okay. "If she admits to the prostitution, we can make an unexpected bust." Might as well gather as much information as possible since the sheriff insisted on having her work for the department.

"How do you like the nightclub?" Moreno stopped at their table, frowning at the sight of the water glasses. "Do you three ever let loose?"

Sheriff Westbrook's smile didn't reach his eyes. "This is letting loose."

Moreno's face darkened, but a smile fit back into place. "Enjoy yourselves. Consider having a beer, at least. They're free tonight."

A beer did sound good to Graham. "I'll get us three," he said after the other man left. "You did say not to attract attention."

"Agreed." Sheriff Westbrook finished his water.

Graham detoured past the table where Gemma sat. "You look beautiful tonight."

She glanced up, pleasure shining in her dark eyes. "You clean up nice, too. So, what do you think of all . . . this." Gemma waved her arm.

"Classy as far as nightclubs go, I guess. I'm not one to frequent such places. You doing okay?"

She hitched her chin. "Yeah, I'm fine. I'm in a lovely house surrounded by expensive luxuries. What could possibly be wrong?"

"You don't have to do this." He felt like a stuck record.

"Too late now. Don't worry about me, Graham. I'm making plans. Will I see you at the diner tomorrow?"

"Absolutely. I'll be there every day you work." Catching sight of Moreno's shrewd expression, he continued to the bar and ordered three of the most expensive beers they carried.

"You interested in my Gemma, Deputy?"

The hair on the back of his neck stood at attention.

Chapter Ten

As if she hadn't felt dirty enough the night before, Gemma now stood in front of Anthony steeling herself for a lecture. "You summoned, my lord?"

"Don't be impertinent." He made a great show of setting his coffee mug on the table. "Why did you stop the girls from taking men to the back rooms?"

Because she hated the thought. "The law was present."

"Perhaps you worried about what Deputy O'Connor would think." He tilted his head. "The two of you seem to be particularly friendly with each other."

"He's a good friend of my aunt's. He looks out for her." She smoothed her work apron. "I'm going to be late, Anthony."

"Not very." The smile he gave sent ice water down her spine. "I've a surprise for you. Since I don't feel I can fully trust you . . . at least not yet. I've brought in someone to help." He slid to his feet and opened the door that connected his office with his bedroom.

Gemma's knees weakened as her old Nanny Rosa entered the room. She fell into a chair. "Why?"

"Because this woman means even more to you than your aunt." Anthony's chilly smile faded. "She will go with you everywhere. To the diner, to the store, to your aunt's house … she will sleep on a twin bed in your room. Failure to comply will not end well for either of you." He shrugged. "Besides, we're going to need a nanny when our baby comes."

Rosa's wide eyes pleaded with Gemma. She might have been a nanny for an Italian family but not an Italian mob. The woman looked as if she'd die of fright right there.

Drawing courage from the deepest part of herself, Gemma pushed to her feet and wrapped the older woman in a hug. "I am so glad to see you."

Rosa's shoulders shook with sobs. "I am so sorry."

"No need to be." She shot Anthony such a look of hatred it surprised her that he didn't wither under the heat of her glare.

Instead, he laughed. "Pregnancy has given you some piss and vinegar. I actually think it's adorable. See you after work. Robert is waiting downstairs." He planted a kiss on her cheek before leaving the room.

Gemma swiped her hand across her cheek. "It's going to be okay, Rosa. I promise. Would you really turn against me?"

"Never." She cupped Gemma's cheeks. "You will tell me what to say each day. We're in this together."

Tears sprang to Gemma's eyes. "I have missed you." She took Rosa's hand. Together, they descended the stairs and out the front door to the waiting car.

Robert held the back-seat door open. "Ladies."

Gemma slid in without acknowledging him. Once Rosa was inside, Robert slid behind the wheel and drove to the diner.

As soon as they entered, Gemma settled Rosa at a

table for two near the kitchen, then she went in search of Lucy. She found her as she came from the cooler. "I'm so sorry I'm late. I had to wait for my babysitter."

"Your what?" Her aunt's brow furrowed.

"Anthony brought in my old nanny to watch over me and let him know if I don't follow the rules."

"That's barbaric!" Her eyes widened.

"Don't worry. Rosa won't betray me." She hoped Anthony wasn't holding something over the woman's head.

"You can trust her?"

"I think so." Gemma smiled. "You'll like her. Her name is Rosa." She headed back to the front to wait on customers.

By the time Graham and Joey came in, Gemma was sitting with Rosa and eating a BLT with cream cheese and French fries. Gemma leaned forward. "The dark red-haired one is Graham O'Connor. He helped me when I first arrived here. Saved my life, actually by fishing me out of the river. The other one is his partner, Joey Hudson. They come in here every day to find out what I can tell them about the Morenos."

Rosa gasped. "That is dangerous, niña."

"I won't let him be in this child's life." She took a big swallow of her drink. "Lunch is over. I have another three hours before my shift is done."

"I will be fine." Rosa took out her knitting.

Gemma approached the booth where the deputies sat, order pad in hand. "Good afternoon. You're a little later than usual."

"Had to check out an abandoned house. Druggies been making themselves at home." Graham smiled up at her. "How are you?"

"Starting to feel the baby." Gemma grinned. "I'm more tired by the end of the day." She lowered her voice. "Anthony has my old nanny shadowing me." She motioned to Rosa. "I feel as if I can trust her, but if you could look into the years between when I entered college and now, I'd appreciate it. Her name is Rosa Garcia."

"Won't be hard to do." Graham crossed his arms, his gaze holding Gemma's. "Is there prostitution going on at the nightclub?" He kept his voice barely above a whisper.

"Yes." Her face heated. "I stopped it last night, but Anthony was furious. I won't be able to again."

"We'll make a bust."

"I'm sure Anthony has a plan to make sure you don't find anything. I'll see what I can discover. What can I bring you?" She asked the question a bit louder.

The men both ordered the day's special of chicken fried chicken. "Be very discreet, Gemma." Graham's concerned eyes spoke volumes.

"I will." She went to turn in the order, aware of Graham's lingering gaze. Did he have feelings for her? Gemma took a moment to ponder that. Did he care more for her than as a friend? The thought had come to mind more than once, but this time she met his gaze to get the answer to her question.

One corner of his mouth curled, then the other, giving her a smile that stopped her heart.

~

Graham's grin widened at the look on Gemma's face. A look that said she'd finally grasped his feelings. Since her eyes didn't harden the way they had before, he had hope that she'd come to feel the same way about him as he did about her.

"Hey, lover boy. Attention back to your job. She isn't it anymore." Joey laughed.

Gemma would aways be "it" for him. "So, you want to do a stakeout at the drug house?"

"Stakeouts are boring, but yeah." Joey straightened when Gemma returned with mugs and a coffeepot.

She smiled as she poured his cup but didn't speak.

Joey, with a grin that took up his whole face, glanced from her to him and back to her. The idiot.

Gemma blushed and moved to the next table.

Graham felt as if his smile would never leave his face until his eyes landed on Rosa. Was the shrewd look on her face more than concern for the woman she raised? Or was it wariness, suspicion, distrust?

The woman would have to get used to him. He might not be at Gemma's side as often as he was before Moreno showed up, but he would be at every opportunity. He raised his mug in a toast to her, chuckling when she averted her eyes.

"Horrible thing—a man distrusting his woman," Joey said. "In this case, Moreno is justified. Let's hope Gemma's deception doesn't get discovered."

"Amen to that."

Later that evening, a little after ten, Graham picked Joey up in his truck before driving to a dirt road half a mile from the drug house. "We'll hoof it from here. Won't catch anyone if they hear us coming."

Joey grunted. "Of course."

"Sorry. I know you aren't stupid." Graham put a finger to his lips and unhooked the clip on his holster. He could be a little heavy-handed at times.

They moved through the woods like ghosts, blending into the shadows. Graham put his hand up to halt Joey a few times to have the opportunity to listen.

Nothing but nature sounded until about ten minutes into their hike. Voices and laughter rang through the trees. The fools weren't even trying to be secretive. Graham glanced around. No lights flickered from a neighboring house—too far away to see and hear anything from the drug house.

Graham moved forward counting four young men waving beer bottles around. Someone shouted from inside the house about needing to make a call. He needed to see inside to get a head count.

"Call for backup," he whispered. "We aren't taking any chances. Pull back."

They melted into the shadows to wait.

"Sheriff says Johnson and Young are on a call. Determine whether these people are armed and decide whether to proceed on our own." Joey clicked his phone.

Not an easy task. "I'll sneak around the side. You keep an eye on the men outside."

When they again approached the house, only two men stood outside.

"Heard we've got a new dealer," one of them said.

"Yeah. Have to go to the side door of what used to be the video rental place. No more street corners. Ain't high class enough, the old dealer said. He's furious." The other shook his head. "You think them New Yorkers are behind all the changes?"

"Yep. Things are about to get real around here."

Whatever that meant. Graham pointed to his right. "When you hear my whistle, step out and apprehend those guys. Bring them into the house. It'll be easier to contain them until we can get a squad car here."

Joey nodded and fixed his gaze on the two men.

Graham stayed low, moving as quickly as possible before emerging from the trees out of sight of the men outside. He darted to the house, plastered his back against the mildew-stained siding, then peered through the window.

Three men and a teenage girl sat on sleeping bags. Candles flickered around them. Burn holes covered the carpet past its prime. Graffiti decorated the walls. Empty liquor and water bottles littered the floor. Fast-food bags piled up in one corner. The kids had definitely made themselves at home. He didn't spot any weapons other than discarded hypodermic needles.

He slid to the front of the house. The door hung on its hinges. He pulled his weapon, gave a shrill whistle, and entered the house gun at the ready.

Those inside screamed and tried to scramble.

"Do not make me shoot you. Sit down and stay put," he ordered. "Backs against the wall."

Joey brought his two in and had them sit with their friends.

"Heard some talk about a new dealer." Graham lowered his weapon. "Mind telling me about him or her?"

"No idea whether it's a guy or a chick," one of them said, crossing his arms. "Ain't been there yet."

"Then tell me what you do know." There was always one talkative person in any group.

"It's only a guess, but we think the mob is here to take over."

"You're a genius." Graham laughed. "Are they really dealing out of the video rental store?"

"That's what we heard. You going to arrest us?"

"Yep. You're trespassing and using illegal

substances, not to mention I'd wager this young lady isn't eighteen yet. Who's her boyfriend?" None of them answered, but the girl's eyes settled on the young man next to her who had to be at least twenty. "We'll have rides soon, so sit tight. If you've any illegal substance on your person, remove it and any paraphernalia to the center of the floor. One at a time."

It didn't take long for a small pile to form. Every one of them carried something they shouldn't. "Y'all are ruining your lives. You know that, don't you?" He shook his head hoping they'd be sent to rehab and praying it would work.

After an hour, Johnson and Young showed up with a van. Once the group was taken, Graham secured the house with crime-scene tape until they could clear the place, then he headed through the woods with Joey toward his truck.

Inside, he turned the key in the ignition. "Moreno is going to try and turn Misty Hollow into a ring of crime."

"Looks that way. Lots of money in the type of crime he does."

The man wouldn't be easy to stop, but Graham would do his best, even if it was the last thing he did as deputy.

Chapter Eleven

Anthony stared out the open front doors of the nightclub as a multitude of leather-wearing bikers roared into the parking lot. The club's bouncers flanked him on both sides, their presence helping to release some of the tension in his back and shoulders. He'd been expecting this day. Anthony plastered a smile on his face. "I'm sorry, boys, but we're not open yet."

The biggest man he'd ever seen rolled his Harley to within a few feet of Anthony. "We wouldn't step foot in this trashy place if you paid us. But, we do want our hangout back. Go back to New York where you came from, Mr. Moreno. We don't take to your kind here."

Anthony sneered. "And what kind am I?"

"Scum. Filth. Getting rich on dirty money. Bringing drugs and prostitution into our town. We've dealt with organized crime before, and the sheriff run them off. He'll do the same with you."

"We'll see. Put on a suit sometime and come in and enjoy yourself." Anthony stepped back while his men closed the doors. Time to involve his father. He headed to his office and made the call.

"How's the small town treating you?" His father laughed.

"A group of would-be hero bikers are getting in my way. I need more men."

"You want to start a war?"

"If need be." Nothing would come between him and his goal of building an empire of his own. Something away from his father's holdings. It rankled that he had to make this call in the first place.

"Anywhere suitable to stay?"

"A few places to rent or buy, but most would have to stay in neighboring towns."

"Well, that won't do. Find a place to accommodate a large number of men and give me a call back." His father hung up.

Anthony cursed then called Lisa, his mistress and realtor, to explain what he needed. "I need it like yesterday."

"There is nowhere in Misty Hollow that fits that description."

"If it needs work, I'll take care of that." He could hear her tapping her nails.

"There's an old nursing home that might work, but it's expensive. That's why it's still empty."

He took a deep breath to tamp down his anger. "That's exactly what I'm looking for. Make sure it's furnished, that everything works, and hire kitchen and cleaning staff. Make it happen now." How he wished for an old-fashioned phone so he could slam down the receiver. A vacant nursing home wouldn't be fancy, but it was good enough for hired men.

He called his father back. "I found a place, but it will take a few days to make it suitable."

"You'll have the men you require by next week's end." He hung up.

Anthony rubbed his hands together. He'd now have the necessary force to rid Misty Hollow of the bikers, the sheriff, and the two-bit deputies. Then he'd bring in his own law enforcement and build the mountain town into something huge.

~

"Heard the biker group paid a visit to your fiancé." Wilbur, a regular at the diner's counter, dipped his toast in the top of his over-easy egg.

"Well? Don't leave me hanging." Gemma refilled his coffee cup. "What happened?"

"I wasn't there. How would I know?"

She laughed. "You know everything."

"What I will tell you is—it can't be good. Lines are being drawn in the sand, so to speak." His gaze met hers. "You be careful now, ya hear?"

"I'll do my best." His concern filled her with warmth as she moved to the next customer.

"I don't like hearing that," Lucy said, moving past her with a tray of dirty dishes. "There's Dave right now. Go find out what in the heck is going on."

Gemma glanced to where the big biker squeezed into a booth. She nodded and headed his way with a clean coffee cup. "Good morning, Dave."

"Mornin', Miss Gemma." His eyes trailed to her stomach. "Baby growing just fine?"

"Yes, sir. He or she will be a rowdy one." She filled his cup. "Heard tell you paid a visit to Moreno."

He gave a slow nod. "Word travels fast in this town. We want him out of here, no offense to you."

"None taken." Gemma bent low. "I want him gone, too." She smiled and clapped his shoulder. "But, you've disturbed a fire anthill. He won't take to that kindly."

"Me and the boys ain't afraid of him." His eyes flashed, and his face darkened. "He's ruining this peaceful town."

Unfortunately, Anthony was just getting started. "Just be careful, please." Gemma smiled as Graham, minus Joey, entered the diner. She excused herself and followed him to his usual booth. "Solo today?"

"Joey's under the weather." He waved away the offer of a menu. "I'll take the special. A burger sounds good." He glanced at Dave who waved at him, then he sighed.

"Worried?" Gemma asked.

"Yep."

"I'm sorry I don't have anything to report today. Anthony has been involved in that resort on the mountain, and he's gone quite a bit." And that was just fine with her. "He hasn't even asked Rosa if I'm behaving." She laughed, glancing to where the woman sat at the table near the kitchen reading a book. "She's bored out of her mind."

"Why not ask Lucy to hire her? She could wait tables and still keep an eye on you."

"That's a good idea." Gemma wondered how much Anthony paid her to be a watchdog. "Do you know she stands outside the bathroom when I'm in there? It's annoying."

"I've heard that babies and dogs are the same." He grinned.

She laughed. "So have I. Guess Rosa is my practice run. I'll place your order."

After she added it to the metal ring, Gemma stood by Rosa's table. "Would you like to work at the diner? I'm sure Lucy could use your help."

Closing her book, Rosa glanced up wide-eyed. "Really? Mr. Moreno is paying me very well to watch you. He would not be happy."

"Well, you wouldn't have to tell him. You're here with me every day anyway."

She stared at Gemma for a moment. "Yes, please ask your aunt. Also, I need to tell Mr. Moreno something. He's getting suspicious about you being good all the time." She smiled. "Guess he knows you too well."

"I'll think of something before we head home." Something minor that wouldn't result in too strict of discipline. She was far from ready to become his prisoner.

Why couldn't she find more information on Anthony? Something that would benefit law enforcement? After that first night, he hadn't allowed her to come to the club after opening hours. The only part she played was meeting with the girls on her day off from the diner, so she had no idea how Anthony would protect what happened in the back rooms if a raid occurred on the club.

She needed to step up her game of nosiness. Gemma eyed Rosa, the only person in the house she could reasonably trust. Suspecting her room and bathroom were most likely bugged, she needed a different place to have the discussion with her. "Come to the bathroom with me."

Rose scowled. "Aren't you a little old for that?"

"Come on." Gemma grabbed her hand, dragging her with her.

In the restroom, she made sure they were alone then locked the door. "I need help finding something on Anthony to put him behind bars."

"There's a lot of things, *mia*." She crossed her arms.

"Proving it is what I need."

"Ask your deputy friend. I don't have the mind for this."

She couldn't ask Graham. He'd already made clear how he felt about the sheriff wanting her help. "Please."

"I could take the cleaning girl's place on your next day off. She doesn't speak a lick of English and would do anything for money. Then I'll nose around."

Gemma chewed her nail. "I'd rather I be the one nosing around. I don't want you in trouble."

"Speaking of—" Rosa wiggled her fingers. "Give me something to tell the man."

Gemma thought for a moment. "I've been too vocal with you about the nightclub. Anthony won't like that I'm not supporting him in his endeavors. How about you mention I feel the same about the resort." That shouldn't get her into too much trouble, right?

~

Graham waited with the sheriff, Johnson, and Young outside the club. Tonight, they hoped to bring down Anthony's prostitution ring. Since Gemma hadn't been able to find out how the man had always escaped arrest, they'd be going in blind.

When the sheriff gave the signal, the four of them rushed to the back door. Graham and Westbrook pressed their backs to the wall while Johnson opened the door, gun at the ready.

No cries of alarm came from inside. He continued, the rest following.

They entered a hallway with doors on each side. A soft light lit the space.

Sheriff Westbrook reached for the closest door

handle and turned. Instead of opening, an alarm blared from another room.

Graham stared wide-eyed at the others. A distraction? Or could the doors only be opened from the inside or with a key? The alarm continued to blare. He pressed his ear to the door. On the other side came sounds of hushed words and scuffling then nothing. "They managed to get away."

"Hidden tunnel?" Young asked, her face creased with worry. "Should we leave? We're sitting ducks."

"Retreat," Westbrook barked, heading for the back door. "We'll go through the front next time."

Graham couldn't help but be impressed with Moreno's ingenuity. Did the alarm sound only in the rooms or also in the main part of the building? If the alarm sounded throughout the entire building, why hadn't anyone come to confront them?

Movement in the trees alerted him to the fact they weren't alone. "Sheriff." Graham motioned to where several bikers congregated in the shadows.

"Are you kidding me?" The sheriff marched toward them. "Mind telling me what's going on, Dave?"

"We're here to cause some trouble." He slapped an iron bar against his palm.

"Do you realize that those inside will be using guns?" He snatched the bar from the man's hand. "Don't be a fool. The only way to Moreno is through the law. Being a thug will get you killed."

Footsteps crunched behind them. Graham whirled, gun in hand.

Moreno held up his hands. "Don't shoot. I heard about a ruckus out here. What's going on, Sheriff?"

"Everything is under control." The sheriff glared at

Dave. "Just running off some of your unwelcome company."

"That all?" Moreno glanced around the deputies.

"That's it."

Graham lowered his weapon. The man didn't act as if he knew they'd been inside, but he could be a good actor.

Moreno and Dave were engaged in a staring contest, neither man backing down.

Graham glanced at the sheriff. "What now?" He mouthed.

"These men are trespassing, Sheriff." Moreno tilted his head. "I told them earlier today not to come around again."

"You did not. You told us to put on suits!" Dave took a step forward.

"Dave, take your boys out of here before I haul all of you to jail for trespassing." He turned to Moreno. "We'll handle this. Go back inside."

"I'm going to press charges."

"Then come to the office tomorrow and do just that." The sheriff waved Dave and his men away.

"I want a restraining order."

"Fine with me." Sheriff Westbrook motioned his head for the deputies to follow him as Dave and his buddies headed back the way they'd come.

Graham glanced over his shoulder and met the stony gaze of Moreno.

Chapter Twelve

After three days of being locked in her room for asking questions, Gemma couldn't wait to get to the diner. This whole disaster with Anthony showing up in Misty Hollow left Lucy in a bind. Not to mention the baby was due in five months.

"Ready?" She turned to Rosa who proudly sported her own yellow frilly apron.

She smiled, nodded, and opened the front door.

Gemma's heart fell to her knees at the sight of Anthony Moreno, Senior.

He frowned, raking cold eyes over her and Rosa. "Where are the two of you going?"

"To work." Gemma squared her shoulders. "Anthony is permitting me to work for a few more months. It keeps me from going stir-crazy."

He blinked a few times then marched past her muttering something about all women being crazy. "Where's my son?"

"Last room on the right." She rushed out the door before he called her back. Having him here was not good. Not good at all.

She didn't need to tell Robert where to take them. The aprons said it all. Gemma chewed her thumbnail, her brain whirling. Why was Anthony Senior in town? His being here could very well mean he'd brought a bunch of men with him. Was he going to start a war? If so, with whom? Gemma longed to tell her driver to stop at the sheriff's office so she could speak with Graham, but the repercussions would be severe. Having Anthony trust her grew harder and harder. She slouched in the seat and tossed Rosa a dejected look. Would she ever be free of the mob?

The other woman reached over and gave her hand a squeeze. "It will be fine." She smiled.

Gemma hoped so.

"When is your shift over?" Robert peered in the rearview mirror.

"Three."

He nodded and got out of the car to open the rear door. "I'll be here at five 'til. The boss has something planned."

Rolling her eyes, she slid from the car. She wouldn't punch out until three on the dot. It didn't matter what Anthony had planned. She hung her purse in the back room and grabbed her order pad before waiting on Wilbur. "Wouldn't be a good day without seeing you here."

"I agree." He grinned. "Missed you the last three days."

"One day was my day off. The other day I wasn't . . . feeling well." She forced a smile.

"They opened up the old nursing home." After she poured his coffee, he added two creams and two sugars. "I saw a lot of men going in. Men who didn't look old enough to be in a nursing home."

The hand holding the pot trembled so hard she set

the pot on the counter. "Maybe they were construction workers."

He shook his head. "Construction workers don't wear suits. You know, my place is right on the other side of the fence bordering that property. I saw them pushing in crates. A few women in white aprons climbed out of a white van. It could all be on the up-and-up, but something fishy is going on. I always trust my gut."

Gemma agreed. Something was definitely not right. If Anthony Senior hadn't arrived, she might not have been as worried. She jerked her head for Graham to meet her in the short hallway that led to the storage room. This information was too important to be overheard.

A pleased look crossed his face as he followed her. "Am I finally going to get to kiss you?"

She widened her eyes. "Not while I'm carrying Anthony's child."

His brow furrowed. "Why not? It isn't as if you love him."

"It doesn't feel right. Concentrate, Graham." Although she couldn't help the rush of happiness that enveloped her at knowing he wanted to kiss her.

"I think the Morenos are using the old nursing home for something." She filled him in on what Wilbur had told her. "That isn't the worst part, though. Anthony Senior is in town."

His features hardened. Gone was the flirtatious gleam in his eyes. "That doesn't bode well for this town."

She gripped his arm. "Graham, I think he's bringing in an army."

"Why?"

"Because he'll need one to take over this town." She reached up in a rare moment of fondness and cupped his cheeks. "I'm scared for you. You aren't the sort to back down. He'll try to bribe you, threaten you, then kill you."

The corner of his mouth quirked. "I'm not as easy as all that, sweetheart." He planted a soft kiss on her forehead. "I've got to go. Be careful."

With her heart in her throat, she kept her gaze on his broad back until she couldn't see him anymore. Blinking back tears, she went back to work with a resolve to risk everything to dig deeper into what Anthony was planning.

~

Anthony watched as his father strolled the halls and rooms of what was now their headquarters. At least in Misty Hollow. "There's a room for everyone. I know it isn't up to our standards regarding luxury, but it'll suffice until we get there."

His father turned a hard stare on him. "Why this town? There's nothing here."

"It's the perfect place to start from the ground up. There isn't much here now, but within a few years, I'll own an empire worthy of leaving to my child." He puffed out his chest. "I don't want to live in your shadow forever."

"Good. I didn't raise a lazy son." He glanced around. "Where's my office?"

Anthony led him to the largest nonessential room in the place, the room he'd chosen for himself. "We can knock out a door next door if you want."

"This is fine. I'll have furniture brought in. Don't worry, I don't plan on infringing on your business. We'll share this office. Now show me your plans." He sat in a hard chair next to a square metal table.

Anthony pulled a large binder from the top of a

cabinet and set it in front of him. "Plans for the resort and ideas for the rest of the town. The whole place needs a facelift, don't you think?"

"Hmm." His father flipped through the binder. "Can the local law enforcement be bought?"

"I don't think so. The sheriff is a real hard nose, and one of his deputies . . . well, he seems a little too interested in Gemma."

"Well, take care of him." His father glanced up. "This town will either be with you or against you. Take care of those who are against you." He slapped the binder closed. "You can be lord over this place if you do things the right way. Don't be soft, Anthony. Not even with Gemma."

He nodded as if in agreement. One thing Anthony would do differently than his father. His son or daughter would never have to wonder whether he loved them for themselves or to just keep the empire going.

~

Sheriff Westbrook rubbed his chin. "You and Hudson head out there. See what's going on. I'm sure everything will look legal. Try to get a good look at Senior Moreno. Find out if he plans on sticking around."

Nodding, Graham stood. "Will do." He left and found Joey in the breakroom staring at a box of doughnuts. "You know those are a few hours old, right?"

"Yeah, but there's a chocolate one left. My favorite."

"So, eat it." He grinned.

"Trying to watch my calories." He closed the box. "I've seen too many overweight cops and, with the Morenos in town, I need to stay fit."

"Speaking of . . . we need to pay a visit to their

newest location."

Joey followed him to the squad car. "I'm sick of these guys. I took the job in this town because I heard it was peaceful."

"It looks peaceful, but this town has had its share of crime." Graham slid into the driver's seat. He drove to the edge of town and parked on the side of the street. The amount of comings and goings from the horseshoe-shaped building left him on edge. This many people definitely looked like an army to him. Several had guns strapped to their waists. "Keep your wits about you." Graham shoved his door open and headed toward the building.

A man entering the building shot him a glance then rushed inside. Seconds later, both Moreno men stood in the doorway.

"Deputies, welcome."

"To what, exactly?" Graham narrowed his eyes at a man who stepped close behind the Morenos.

"This is where my men will live as we build the resort." Moreno grinned. "There's no hotel to speak of, and why leave a building vacant when it can serve a purpose?"

"And after the resort?"

"We'll have to wait and see. Deputy, meet my father."

Graham simply nodded rather than offer his hand as he would any other man. "You sticking around long?"

The older man's smile didn't meet his eyes. "I'm leaving in the morning. My son seems to have everything under control. Mind walking with me for a minute, Deputy?"

Joey's eyes widened. "I don't think—"

"Sure. I'll take a tour." Graham motioned for Joey to remain outside. He didn't expect the man to shoot him in broad daylight.

Moreno led him into the dining room before facing him. "Heard you're interested in Miss Ricca."

"That doesn't sound wise, now, does it?" Graham crossed his arms. "Following around after Anthony Moreno's woman? Sir, I'm not that foolish." *Oh, but he was.*

"I certainly hope not." His narrow eyes searched Graham's face. "For your sake."

Graham arched a brow. "Are you threatening me?"

"Not at all." The man clapped him on the shoulder. "Have a good day, Deputy. Consider joining my son in leading this town."

Not in a million years. After a stare down of several seconds, Graham marched back outside. "Come on, Joey."

"What did you find out?"

He whirled. "That they're going to try and get us on the payroll. If you turn dirty, I will punch you in the face."

Joey paled. "I would never."

Maybe not, but some would. There would be law enforcement coming from other cities to take the money. Graham and Joey wouldn't last long once that happened. They'd have a target on their back as big as the town's water tower.

They returned to the office to fill the sheriff in. "Won't be the first time someone has tried to bribe him," he said. "If you two want to leave town while you can, go on. I'd rather you leave than turn."

"I don't plan on leaving." Graham hitched his chin.

"I'm in for the long haul. This town means too much to me." The town and a certain dark-haired woman.

"I'm not leaving either," Joey said. "Even if I thought this would be a cushy job."

The other two laughed, then Graham sobered at the task ahead. "What's the plan?"

"Keep trying to find something concrete to take them down. We'll find it. And we'll find a way to help NYPD pin Esposito's murder on Junior. Leave his father to New York. Then, we'll shut this whole operation down and reclaim our town."

Sounded good, but there wasn't a plan. They simply had to wait for Moreno to mess up. Something Graham didn't think he did very often. If he did, his father cleaned up the mess.

"Keep your eyes and ears open, Gentlemen. Good night." The sheriff trudged past them as if he carried the weight of the world on his shoulders. He actually did, at least his small part of it. Graham was glad Misty Hollow was in his hands. If there was a way to win this, Sheriff Westbrook would find it and use Graham and the other deputies to help.

He looked forward to bringing Moreno down and prayed no one died in the process.

Chapter Thirteen

Having taken the grave risk of discovery, Gemma paid a cleaning woman a lot of money to "forget" to lock Anthony's office door. Now, she stared at a sketch of what she believed to be Misty Hollow, now almost unrecognizable.

A massively grotesque resort marred the mountaintop. Nightclubs and restaurants replaced the quaint shops on Main Street. A few miles from the city's outer edge sat a casino. Anthony planned on taking over the entire town and turning it into a den of iniquity. A den that would make him very, very wealthy. His plans would bring evil to Misty Hollow such as none the city had seen before.

How could anyone stop him? She sagged against the desk. Not her. She didn't have the resources and doubted even Graham and Sheriff Westbrook would be able to be anything more than a gnat fluttering in front of Anthony's face.

She hurried from the office after turning the lock and pulled the door closed. She'd speak to Graham at the diner. At least, they could cause enough distractions to slow Anthony down until they could figure out how to stop him.

As Robert drove her and Rosa to the diner, Gemma stared out the window. Already the town's atmosphere had changed. Mingled with coveralls and simple country clothing were suits and scantily dressed women strolling the sidewalks. Tears pricked her eyes.

This was her fault. Gemma should never have come. She should leave. But if she did, Anthony would follow. She'd make a plan to flee as far away from Misty Hollow as possible. Away from Graham and Aunt Lucy. Something that would put a knife through her heart.

The morning passed in a daze as she worked on autopilot. When Graham waltzed in, he crooked his finger for her to follow him. Glancing around, he ducked into the stockroom. When she entered, he backed her against the wall.

"Good morning." His greeting wafted over her. "Is today the day you let me kiss you?"

Leaving him would be so hard. She planted her hands flat against his muscular chest. "Not today, you idiot." Gemma laughed, then sobered, and filled him in on what she'd discovered in Anthony's office.

"You sure know how to kill the romance." He backed away.

"I'm worried, Graham. What if we can't stop him?"

"We will." His eyes flashed. "With you in that cursed house, we already know more than we would have without you."

They wouldn't have even that help once she left.

"I hate that the sheriff is having you snoop, but it is helpful." His gaze clashed with hers. "Do I want to know how you got this information?"

"I bribed a cleaning lady not to lock the office door."

"Whoa." The word left him in a rush. "I hate this."

Pain creased his face. "What if that woman tells him?"

She shrugged. "I'll face that if it happens."

Rosa entered the room. "Come. Mr. Moreno's men are waiting to give their order and asked for you. You shouldn't be here with him." She shot Graham a stern look.

"I'm passing on information. Wait a few minutes, okay?" She asked Graham.

He nodded. "I won't do anything to jeopardize you."

Gemma left the stockroom and rushed to wait on three men in dark suits. If she didn't know any better, she'd assume they were secret service or FBI. "What can I get you gentlemen?"

"It took you long enough," one said.

"A pregnant woman visits the restroom a lot." She pasted on a smile.

"The boss wants to know what's the best this place has to offer."

"It's all quite good, even if it isn't fancy."

Nodding, he glanced at the menu. "Steak and eggs."

The other two said they'd have the same.

As Gemma turned to give the chef the order, Graham came down the hall wiping his hands on some paper towels. He made a beeline for the booth where Joey sat without glancing her way.

A few minutes after delivering Moreno's men's food, the only one who seemed to have a voice requested to speak with both Lucy and the chef in private.

"I'll take you to the kitchen." Ice gripped her heart. She shot Graham a worried look as she passed.

"Lucy, this gentleman would like to speak with you and the chef." Gemma started to leave but changed her mind. She wanted to know what would transpire.

"Mr. Moreno is looking for a place for his men to gather," the man said with no expression on his face. His tone left no room for argument. "The food is filling and tasty even if it has no flair. This will be the place. You will be tipped generously each time."

"I can put flair in food." Chef Rawlings frowned. "I went to culinary school. Top of my class."

"Absolutely not." Lucy crossed her arms, a storm crossing her eyes. "This is a family diner. Your kind is not welcome here."

"If you refuse, you'll have no diner."

Gemma gasped. They'd destroy the place. Her aunt's livelihood would be gone.

Lucy's eyes stared a hole into his head. "I've a back room I can set up for y'all. A private room. You'll enter through the back."

"I'll return in a second." He came back a few minutes later. "I need to see this room."

Gemma followed as her aunt led him to a room sometimes rented for wedding receptions—a large plain room that could be transformed into almost anything.

"Here it is. Any furniture or decorating will have to come out of your boss's pocket. I'm not paying for it."

"This will do." His lips twitched as he made another call. When he hung up, he turned his attention back to Lucy. "Rather than individual tickets, Mr. Moreno will rent the room for a nice sum which will include the food, and yes, he will pay for decorating."

Gemma sighed. Why would Anthony need a back room at the diner?

~

Anthony crossed one ankle over his knee and peered at Gemma who stood in front of him. "One of my men said you took a long time in the bathroom this morning and that a few minutes after you returned, so did Deputy O'Connor. What exactly is your relationship with him? Do not lie to me."

She lifted her chin, her gaze locked on his. "When I ran, I turned a corner too fast with my car and plunged into the river. When I managed to get out of the car, the current swept me away. Graham was fishing and came to my rescue. If not for him, I'd be dead."

"If your story is true, I owe him a huge debt of gratitude." He steepled his fingers. "I see how that would form a bond between the two of you, but my darling Gemma, you cannot be friends with the man. It simply isn't right. People will talk."

"Let them. You're Anthony Moreno. No one would dare say anything to your face."

"You do realize how easy it is to verify the accident, right?"

"Of course. I'll show you where the car went in."

He didn't care for her obstinate tone, but at least she cooperated. He'd take what he could get at this point. "You're beginning to show a bit. Your time at the diner is coming to an end."

"I feel fine."

"No one wants to see a pregnant woman." He drew his brows together.

"This is the twenty-first century, Anthony." She crossed her hands over her stomach.

He sighed. "I'll call you tomorrow to show me where your car is." He reached for his phone. "We're finished for now. I require your presence at dinner this evening. My men need to see us as a united front."

He leaned back in his chair, the leather creaking as

he watched her leave. His father would think him too lenient with her. Anthony wanted her as comfortable as possible so nothing would happen to the baby. No stress, no heavy lifting—absolutely nothing to risk the pregnancy. Once his child was born, things would change. Gemma would know her place or suffer the consequences.

"Has the shipment arrived?" He spoke into his phone.

"An hour ago. We're lying low right now. A couple of the deputies were looking our way as we drove the U-Haul into town."

"Good. Don't wait too long, though. There's a lot of money riding on this transaction."

Now, which deputies were causing trouble this time? Anthony hung up. The entire sheriff's department were such a waste of his time.

He smiled. No one could stop a Moreno when they put their mind to something.

~

Graham listened as Johnson stated his suspicion about the U-Haul. "Maybe someone new is arriving in town."

"Possibly, but they weren't driving on residential streets. It warrants checking into." He grabbed his jacket. "I'm off."

"Without checking out your suspicion?"

"Yep. The sheriff thinks the same as you, so why waste my time?"

"I'm not off for another hour. I'll cruise around town and see if I can spot the truck. Goodnight." Graham shut down his laptop and pushed to his feet. If they were going to investigate every little thing, they'd be working twenty-four seven.

As he drove, he couldn't help but dwell on Gemma. Pregnancy suited her. Her skin glowed with good health. Graham couldn't help but wish she carried his child rather than Moreno's. Still, he could pray they'd have a future together once all this was past them. He really wanted to know what it was like to kiss Gemma Ricca.

He slowed spotting the tail end of a U-Haul truck sticking out of the back of an abandoned mall. Graham pulled into the lot and parked behind the truck. His hands gripped the steering wheel as he contemplated his next move.

He pushed open his door and grabbed his weapon from the passenger seat after sending a text to the sheriff. It wouldn't hurt to look around until he heard back.

Using caution, he opened the back door to the building and stepped inside. Dim light filtered through dirty windows of what looked like a fast-food joint long since closed down. He could almost smell the grease.

Graham exited the joint and stepped into the annex. The faint sound of voices appeared to come from what might have been a department store. The building had been set up in the form of an X on the inside with a food court taking up the center which was where Graham stood. He moved forward, freezing when his foot scuffed the marble floor.

"You hear that?" A man's voice asked.

"Nah. Your imagination. If you're so worried, go check it out. I saw a cat earlier."

Graham held his breath, moving again when no one came to investigate.

The cell phone in his pocket rang. He cringed, having forgotten to put the phone on silent. He pulled it from his pocket and sprinted for the closest open door.

Empty clothes racks provided little in the way of a hiding place.

Footsteps pounded in the food court.

Graham quickly put his phone on silent and texted the sheriff that he needed backup. He got an immediate response that help was on the way.

His heart leaped to his throat as the footsteps stopped outside the vacant shop mere inches from where he stood. He held his breath in order to hear better. They were inside.

"Come on out. We know you're in here."

Graham hunkered down lower, using a counter to shield him. It wouldn't take long until they were upon him. He needed to hold out until help arrived.

"Maybe he ran out the back?" someone said.

"Look at the dust on the floor. Whoever it is ran in here."

Graham studied his surroundings. Spotting an opening in the wall, he made a mad dash across the room, staying as low as possible. He dove through the opening as gunfire erupted.

Chapter Fourteen

Graham landed in a small hallway with three doors, one on each side and one at the end. He chose the door at the end.

As he ran, he pulled his cell phone and dialed the sheriff again. "Need backup now! I'm taking fire."

"How many shooters?"

"I've heard two voices." He had no idea whether there were more in other parts of the mall. The building wasn't that big, maybe once having housed twenty stores of various sizes.

"Try to get out of there before you're pinned down. Johnson and Young should be there in five."

Graham hung up and barged through the back door which took him into a dark hallway that stretched along the building with access to multiple stores. Three large doors were padlocked. Drat. They most likely led to the outside, providing employees with access to the dumpsters.

He slowly opened the next door and peered into another shop much like the one he'd just left. Rather than enter, he continued to the end of the hall and exited there, finding himself in the main part of the mall. He could see the food court, but no sign of his pursuers.

Ears peeled, he inched forward, gun at the ready. At the cross junction, he turned right in hopes of exiting the building before he was spotted.

A bullet kicked up a piece of marble at his feet, sending him into a sprint. The doors to the outside now had a thick chain and lock holding them closed. Trapped.

He pivoted and ran back to the center, then turned right again. There had to be a way out. Surely, they hadn't had time to lock every door. If he couldn't get out, help couldn't get in. He needed a place to hole up and ambush the two guys trying to kill him.

He ducked into another shop and skidded to a halt. Bags of white powder lay on every available flat surface. No wonder these guys wanted him dead. A lot of money lay in front of him. Money worth killing for. Major drugs had come to Misty Hollow. This was the last room he wanted to be caught in.

Peering out and seeing no one, he rushed from the room and dashed down a different hallway, taking refuge in the last room on his left. A lone baseball cap sat in the corner of the dusty floor, left behind when the place had been packed up.

He took shelter behind the shop counter and kept a sharp eye on the door. *God, let help come before trouble.*

The scuff of a footstep froze him, his breath lodging in his throat. Graham wasn't a coward by any means, but being trapped and outnumbered left him sweating.

"He can't have disappeared," one of the men said. "We bolted the doors."

"Maybe we missed one. The only windows are the main door and in the roof. He can't get out. Keep looking, or Moreno will have our heads."

Their heads instead of his. Graham held his breath

until they moved on. How long could he wait? He glanced at the screen of his phone. Almost an hour and no—

Glass shattered from the front of the mall. Gunshots rang out.

Graham sprang from his hiding place and raced to his comrades' aid. Johnson and Young took turns shooting through the broken glass panel near the front doors. Graham took up position behind the two thugs who kept up a continuous barrage of bullets as they ran from one shop to the other.

He took aim and struck one in the leg. His next shot took the other mid-body. Both fell, dropping their weapons. He rushed forward and kicked the handguns out of the way as Johnson and Young climbed through the window.

"They have this place locked up like my grandmother's root cellar." Johnson pulled a pair of handcuffs from his belt while Young called for an ambulance.

"There's a whole lot of what I believe to be cocaine in one of the vacant shops." Graham cuffed the man he'd shot in the side, ignoring the cursing. "Shut up. You asked to be shot. Two less scumbags on the streets of Misty Hollow." He dragged the man and propped him against a wall. "Medical aid is on the way." He mirandized them.

Arresting these two and confiscating the drugs were two drops in the bucket compared to what was coming. Graham could feel it in his gut.

The fire department arrived with the paramedics and cut the chain on the door with huge bolt cutters. Once the door opened, paramedics entered and took over with the shooters.

When the sheriff arrived, Graham led him to the stash of cocaine. Sheriff Westbrook whistled. "That's a lot. Good job."

"Johnson is the one who suspected something. I had no intention of getting out of my vehicle until I spotted the U-Haul behind the mall. That seemed suspicious."

"I regret blowing him off. That won't happen again."

"You've a lot on your plate, sir."

"That's no excuse for not believing in my deputies." He pulled his phone from a holder at his waist. "Thanks again, O'Connor. Go on home. I'll take it from here. The report can wait until morning."

Graham wouldn't argue. Exhaustion remained ever present as he lost sleep each night worrying about Gemma. Seeing her at the diner was the highlight of each day. He didn't think he'd survive not seeing her again.

~

Anthony sat at one end of the backseat while Gemma sat on the other as far away from him as the car would allow. He'd promised her a kingdom. Why couldn't she accept him? She'd be a very wealthy woman when they married. Not that she didn't have money of her own, but his funds would put her at the top of the country's wealthiest.

He cut her a sideways glance. Other than the simple clothes she wore to the diner, she still dressed as a woman of her class. Today, a gauzy blouse over loose-fitting linen pants barely showing the signs of pregnancy. "You look beautiful today." He smiled.

"Thank you." She didn't bother glancing his way.

"Have I done something to offend you?"

"Pulling me out to prove I'm not lying is offensive." She stabbed him with a cold glare. "My one day off— and we're out here! Not to mention the drive up the mountain to check progress on the resort."

"You don't need to work, so please do not complain about a choice you made." He turned his attention back to the view outside his window. Anthony actually enjoyed the mountain over concrete. "I can see why you like this place. It'll be even better when all my plans come to fruition."

She whipped sideways to face him. "You're going to ruin the beauty of this place with your neon signs, prostitution, drugs, and who knows what else. Why couldn't you have just let me go?"

"Because you carry my child. You may leave once it's born, but the child will always stay with me." His face heated. "Make sure you understand that."

~

She swallowed past a dry throat. Gemma understood all right. That's why she couldn't waste any more time finding a way out.

The driver rounded the curve at the foot of the mountain.

"Pull over here." She didn't wait for him to open her door. She stepped from the car and into the shade of a tree as a tow truck stopped behind them.

A man in a wetsuit exited the passenger side of the tow truck.

Gemma pointed out the tire tracks from the road to the river. "You should find the car right there unless it washed downriver."

Anthony glanced at her as if she was making up more lies. Let him believe her a liar. What he felt about her had stopped mattering over a month ago.

She sighed and placed her hands over her growing stomach. What an idiot she'd been. Now, her child would suffer because of her mistake.

The diver entered the water. The murkiness soon hid him from view.

Gemma sighed again and studied her nails. Maybe a manicure . . . no. Ridiculous while carrying plates at the diner. She'd chip them in no time.

The diver exited the water. "The car is about fifty yards that way lodged against a tree." He pointed down river.

Gemma smirked and shot Anthony a hard glance. She arched a brow but didn't speak.

"Pull the car out of the river." Anthony marched to the water's edge. "Don't blame me, Gemma. It was a hard tale to believe."

"Why? I took the corner too sharp and ended up in the river. If Deputy O'Connor hadn't spotted me, I'd have drowned. I had no more strength left when the river propped me against a log." She hitched her chin and watched as the tow truck moved positions.

Anthony moved to her side and took her hands in his, searching her face. "I will be forever grateful to Deputy O'Connor, despite the fact I don't like when you're speaking to him. It will give people the wrong idea."

"I don't care what people think. He is my friend." But, each day she wished he could be more than her friend. That couldn't happen as long as Anthony was in her life.

The tow truck hoisted its winch. Water poured from the interior of Gemma's car as it rose. Unfortunate for the expensive vehicle, but she preferred her Volkswagen. She smiled. The little car wasn't as well suited for an infant as a sedan. Her smile faded. Something she didn't have to worry about with Anthony's drivers chauffeuring her around.

"We'll take it to the garage, Mr. Moreno, but I'm pretty sure the car is totaled." The tow truck driver approached carrying a clipboard. He pulled off a sheet of paper. "Come by sometime today or tomorrow to pay the bill."

"I'll send someone immediately."

Gemma recognized the shrewd look on Anthony's face. She'd grown to hate it.

"Do a good business at the garage?"

"Fair amount." The man grinned. "Only garage around."

"Consider selling?"

"No, sir. My daddy started that garage. I aim to pass it on to my son. Have a good day." He strolled back to his truck.

Gemma's heart sank. Anthony would try and take the garage along with everything else. If the business made a profit, he'd steal it from his own mother.

"I don't think the car can be fixed, Gemma," Anthony said. "I'll buy you a new one if you insist."

"If I do drive, I prefer my Beetle."

He rolled his eyes. "You're turning into a hillbilly. Pretty soon, you'll be walking around barefoot and pregnant." His attempt at humor wasn't funny.

Gemma marched back to the Mercedes and climbed into the backseat. Would her suitcase fit in the backseat of her car? She didn't have much, but she'd like to escape with what she'd arrived in town with. Not that her clothes would fit her soon anyway. She could purchase new, but by now, Anthony most likely knew her bank-account numbers. He'd be watching for her to spend when she ran. Gemma groaned. She'd have to make a trip to the bank and pull out as much funds as possible. That would set off an alarm. Someone would tip Anthony off. Still, it couldn't be helped. She'd be at the bank when the doors opened and leave town immediately after making her deposit. At least she'd have a head start.

It would be enough. It had to be.

Tears sprang to her eyes at the thought of leaving Lucy and Graham. Hopefully, they'd understand she would do anything for her child.

Chapter Fifteen

Gemma slipped out the front door at ten minutes until nine a.m., her fist clutching the handle to her rolling suitcase. She raced to her aunt's house, the suitcase wheels clicking along the sidewalk, and retrieved her car. At exactly nine, she strolled into the bank as if she weren't afraid of the hounds of hell on her heels.

"I'm doing the nursery for the baby," she lied, plastering a smile on her face and cupping her rounded stomach. "I'd like to withdraw as much cash as possible."

As if the bank teller was used to wealthy people making outrageous claims, she simply nodded and handed Gemma an envelope of cash. "Thank you for your business."

As if an afterthought, Gemma said, "Oh, and if my fiancé comes in, please don't tell him about the money. Part of it is a surprise for him." She forced a laugh and exited the bank. She'd spent precisely ten minutes inside. Now, she climbed back into her car and drove away from Misty Hollow. Tears blurred the vision in her rearview mirror. *Goodbye, Graham.*

She sniffed, shoving her sadness aside. There'd be

time to grieve later. When she was free.

Where could she go that he wouldn't find her? She drove south thinking maybe she could hide in the big state of Texas. Gemma stopped for lunch in Texarkana. Half an hour later, she crossed the border into Texas and drove west until stopping for the night in a town with no stoplights and one seedy motel.

"One bed, please," she told the motel manager. She paid with cash and took the key before retrieving her suitcase from her car.

Inside the room, she lay flat on her back and stared at a water spot on the ceiling in the shape of Arkansas and let the tears fall.

~

Anthony listened, his face expressionless, as Robert told him about the seizing of cocaine and the shootout at the mall. "Casualties?"

"Both men injured, but that isn't the worst part, sir."

"Well, are you going to keep me in suspense?" He didn't have time to beat around the bush.

"A couple of Esposito's men were spotted at the diner."

That was news he definitely didn't want to hear. "Passing through?"

"No, sir. They were asking about houses to rent."

"This puts a damper on the day."

"There's more."

Anthony fought back a curse. "Do you mind telling me all there is to know without me pulling it from you one fiber at a time?"

The man paled. "It appears Miss Ricca is gone."

"Gone where?"

"Uh . . . she took her suitcase and her car."

Anthony bolted to his feet. "When?"

"According to the tracker, around nine a.m. She stopped at the bank, somewhere in Texarkana, and stopped for the night in a Podunk town in Texas."

"You're just now telling me this?"

"Sir, you had me checking on the men in the mall. It wasn't until I returned and Miss Rosa asked after Miss Ricca that I surmised something was wrong."

The man would pay dearly for the mistake. "Bring the car."

He stormed to his room to change out of the casual clothes he'd donned after his dinner. Anthon had assumed Gemma was working at the diner, and he had been so busy with the building of the resort, he hadn't checked. Not a mistake he'd make again.

Did she really believe he wouldn't put a tracker on her car? Of course, she'd guess there'd be one in the bracelet he'd given her, but Anthony wasn't a man of chance. Idiot woman! It would take valuable time he didn't have to drive all night to bring her home.

He rang Robert. "Forget the car. Get me a chopper!"

Anthony pulled a suit from his closet. He never left the house without wearing one unless he got to play the rare game of golf. Something he was way overdue to play. Dressed as befitting his station in life, he strode to the front room to wait for Robert. An hour later, the man arrived.

"Took some doing, sir, but there is a chopper waiting in a field outside of town."

"Good." As they drove out of town, Anthony mulled over how to punish the faithful Robert. Maybe he'd do nothing if they retrieved Gemma without incident. He'd let the man off with a warning. But, if she got away, he'd pay for his incompetence with his life.

It didn't take a genius to know why the Espositos had arrived. They'd want vengeance for the death of Ricky.

Anthony would have to focus on the new threat and delegate responsibilities for the resort. Gemma's decision to run from him couldn't have come at a worse time. His hands curled into fists. If she were married to his father, she'd receive a beating, but Anthony couldn't strike a woman carrying his child. He'd find another way to discipline her.

"Should be there in an hour, Mr. Moreno. There will be a car waiting to take you to the motel," the pilot said over the headpiece.

"Thank you."

The chopper landed on a dirt road through fields freshly harvested for hay. A dark sedan waited, its headlights off. Whoever Robert had hired knew how to be discreet.

Staying low, Anthony exited the chopper and climbed into the waiting vehicle. He gave the driver the address of the motel and settled against the seat.

With no town to speak of, the drive took mere minutes. "Wait here." Anthony shoved open his door and barged into the manager's office. "Gemma Ricca's room." He waved a hundred-dollar bill.

"I don't have anyone by that name." The man searched his computer.

"Dark hair, pregnant, drives that Volkswagen outside."

"Ah. Room 104." He grabbed the money as if Anthony would change his mind. "Want a key?"

Anthony grinned. "Absolutely."

~

Gemma's eyes snapped open.

A man sat in the one chair in the room.

She bolted upright, a gasp escaping her lips.

"Relax, it's only me." Anthony unfolded from the chair. "Time to go." He gripped her arm and dragged her from the bed. With his other hand, he took her suitcase.

"How did you find me?" His hold dug into her arm.

"Tracker on your car."

"Will someone drive it back?"

"Possibly. I haven't decided." He gave her arm a yank.

Gemma swallowed past the rock in her throat. How could she have been so stupid? Since she hadn't been allowed to drive the car since Anthony's arrival in Misty Hollow, she hadn't thought it important enough to check for a tracker.

Anthony's long stride, fierce grip, and squared shoulders as he shoved her into the backseat of a car told her as clear as the night sky above that she was in big trouble. She cupped her stomach protectively and scooted as far away from him as she could.

"Relax. I won't harm you." Anthony cut her a glance. "What do I need to do to keep you from trying to leave?"

"Nothing. It's too late for that."

"Surely, you knew what my family did for a business when we started dating?" He laughed. "No one could be that naïve."

"Blind is more like it." She had suspected a few times and pushed the thought aside because of Anthony's attention and promises of a life filled with wealth and luxury. Straight from the all-girl's boarding school then into college with no real knowledge of the world . . . well, it hadn't been hard to discount the rumors about the Moreno family.

"Did you ever love me?" A pain she rarely heard in his voice pierced her.

"I thought I did." She wasn't sure if what she'd felt was love. It was nothing like the all-consuming emotion she had when Graham was near.

Anthony sighed. "There's the chopper. Do I need to keep a tight hold on you?"

"I won't run." It did her no good.

The driver opened the back door and helped her out. Her bare feet slapped the dirt road as she trudged toward the waiting chopper and doom.

Back at the house, exhaustion had her dragging her feet. "May I go to my room? I need to shower."

"In a minute." Anthony motioned for her to have a seat in the living room. "We need to discuss your behavior."

"I thought we did that in the car." She sat on the edge of the leather sofa.

"At that time, I didn't know what I would do with you." He towered over her. "I've decided that you will stop working at the diner. It's time for you to focus on making this place a home for our child. That should consume all your waking hours. Any shopping that needs to be done will be with Rosa and Robert. I will not argue about this, Gemma. You sealed your fate by running."

"My aunt needs me."

"She'll have to make do and hire someone to replace you." He smiled. "I am not a cruel man, Gemma. We can go by there on occasion to eat a meal. You may go to your room."

Dismissed and feeling as if she'd been tossed a bone by his offer of dinner at the diner, she headed for the shower to wash the scent of his cologne off her.

~

Graham pulled into the parking lot of the sheriff's department after a day off. He stopped inside at the sight of several young Hispanic men and two white men handcuffed and waiting in plastic chairs.

Doris glanced up from her desk. "The sheriff is waiting for you in the conference room. I've made coffee. You'll need it."

Anxiety about the meeting seemed like a great way to start the day. Graham exhaled and joined the sheriff and the other three deputies in the conference room. "Busy morning?"

"Going to get busier." The sheriff stood at the end of the table. "Those yahoos in there were putting out strips in the road to flatten tires and stop cars. Then, they proceeded to rob the people inside." The sheriff shook his head. "Did it to the wrong few good ole' boys, and here they are."

Graham frowned. "Who would put them up to that?"

"It's an initiation set in place by the Esposito family to find out who was good enough— trustworthy enough—to be one of their minions."

"We now have the Morenos and the Espositos in town?" Graham poured a cup of coffee and left it black. "What do we do? How are we going to control all these young boys with nothing better to do than get in trouble?"

"For one, I'll be calling for help from neighboring cities. We need a more constant presence on the streets.

You'll spend a lot of time in your cars from now on, folks. I want a squad car seen every minute." The sheriff slapped the table. "We will not lose this town."

His words sounded like a call to war. Graham took a swig of too-hot coffee and started choking.

Joey reached over and gave him a few hard pats on the back. "Slow down, slick."

Gemma would be right in the middle of any war, and there was nothing Graham could do about it. Esposito could easily kidnap Gemma and use her and her baby as leverage.

To make the odds even worse after Anthony killed Ricky Esposito, Moreno senior wouldn't hesitate to kill Moreno's child, which meant killing the mother. "We need protective custody on Gemma Ricca and Lucy Romano."

"We can't get close to Miss Ricca. Not after her adventure last night," the sheriff said. "But we can find someone to watch Miss Romano."

Graham stiffened. "What adventure?"

"The gutsy woman tried escaping. Made it to Texas before Moreno found out and brought her back." The sheriff shook his head. "They'll have her locked up and watched every second now."

Graham couldn't help but feel proud as well as worried. At least Gemma had the backbone not to accept her fate without a fight.

He had to find a way to help her.

Chapter Sixteen

For almost a week, she didn't leave the house. From her window, she'd see Graham drive past. She'd place her palm flat against the window and hoped he'd see her. Today, she had a doctor's appointment and wished it was Graham taking her and not Robert.

But, it wasn't to be. She grabbed her purse and headed downstairs to wait for Rosa and Robert. Once in the back seat, she slipped a note into Rosa's hand. "take it to Deputy O'Connor," she whispered.

The other woman nodded and slipped the note into her purse.

The note was to let Graham know that Gemma was okay. Since she didn't know when Anthony would take her to the diner, she couldn't ask Graham to meet her in the hall by the bathrooms. It pained her to realize how much she missed him trying to steal a kiss, and how much she wished she'd have let him.

Robert stayed in the car as Gemma and Rosa entered the clinic. Gemma signed in and took a seat.

The others in the waiting room glared as if it was her fault their town had fallen to the mob. Her shoulders sagged. She fought to keep her head up. Her next appointment would be in Langley where people would be less likely to kill her with their stares.

She straightened as Graham entered, dressed in jeans and a tee-shirt that showed off his muscular arms. His eyes widened at the sight of her. After he signed in, he sat next to her.

"I didn't expect to see you," she said softly. Her day had just brightened.

"Same here. I'm due for my yearly checkup, and the sheriff is adamant we not skip each year." He smiled and leaned close, ignoring the curious looks from the waiting patients. "This isn't the place, but I'd kiss you if you'd let me."

Her face heated and she giggled then clamped a hand over her mouth. "Hush. You'll get me in trouble. Anthony has spies everywhere."

"Even here?"

"Probably." Some of the joy left her.

"I heard you tried to run."

"I did, and now I'm in lockdown until the baby is born." Gemma feared what would happen then. She pulled at a loose button on her blouse. "Anthony loves me in his own way. Things will be okay."

"I'm here if you need me." He stood as a nurse called his name. "All you have to do is send word."

"Here." Rosa thrust the note Gemma had written at him.

"It's telling you I'm okay."

His gaze searched her face. "So, you say, but I've never seen a sadder woman than the one sitting in front of me." He turned and followed the nurse from the room.

A few minutes later, Gemma's name was called, and she followed a nurse to the examination room.

"It's ultrasound day. Do you want to know the

gender?" The nurse had her lay on the bed and unbutton her blouse.

"Yes. The father wants to know."

The nurse squeezed cold gel on Gemma's stomach then pressed a wand against her skin. "Looks like you have a healthy baby boy."

Gemma's heart skipped a beat. Anthony would be ecstatic. Maybe knowing she carried his son would put him in a good enough mood to allow her a little more freedom.

Gunshots sounded outside.

The nurse locked the door and pulled down a shade. "Please move off the table and into the far corner of the room, Miss Ricca."

An alarm sounded as the clinic went into lockdown.

Someone pounded on the room where Gemma and the nurse hid.

"Gemma!"

"It's the deputy." She started for the door.

"Do not open that door." The nurse shot out a hand to stop her.

"We're okay, Graham," she called out. "Be careful."

"I will." Pounding footsteps signaled him running from the door.

Gemma glanced around the room for a weapon in case the shooter came inside. She found nothing but a metal tray. The ultrasound room was definitely not a place to fight anyone off.

She dug her phone from her purse and glanced at the screen. No signal. "Is there a phone in here?"

"Yes." The nurse retrieved a desk phone from a cupboard and plugged it in. "We don't use cell phones in here because of the interference."

Realizing Graham had most likely called the sheriff's department already, she dialed Anthony.

"Anthony Moreno."

"It's me, Gemma. Someone is shooting outside the clinic. We're pinned down inside. The only gun we have is Deputy Graham's."

"The deputy is there?"

"Doctor's appointment. It's the only clinic in town." She couldn't keep the frustration from lacing her words. "Help us."

"I'll send men. Stay safe." He hung up.

Gemma hated asking him for help, but if anyone could get rid of the shooter outside, it would be his men. She leaned her head against the wall. A few minutes later, what sounded like a war started outside. It lasted only a few minutes, then another knock sounded at the door.

"It's me," Graham said. "You're okay to come out."

Gemma rushed for the door, pulled it open, and wrapped her arms around Graham's waist. "Thank you."

He peeled her off him. "Don't thank me." He jerked his head toward Anthony.

"Thank you." She stepped in front of Anthony. "We're having a boy."

His face split into a grin. "This calls for a celebration."

"Not yet, Mr. Moreno." Graham joined them. "Gemma was the target here. Your enemies thought they could get to her at the clinic. It isn't safe for her to be out."

He nodded. "She'll be safe enough in the house. We'll celebrate privately. Again, I am in your debt." He put his hand on the small of Gemma's back and led her from the clinic.

She glanced back one last time at the face of the man she wanted but couldn't have.

~

Anthony almost forgot the sight of Gemma in the deputy's arms at the news they'd have a son, but then it came back. "You really don't listen to me, do you?"

Her eyes flicked to the bodies on the ground, the bullet ridden car, and Robert's lifeless body. "About what?"

"Your behavior around the deputy." He opened the rear door to his car. "This is Nicco. He's your driver now."

"I was overcome by emotion, Anthony. People are dead, and I find out one of them should be me."

"I promise not to let that happen." He closed the door and motioned for Nicco to lower the window. When he did, he said, "Straight home, Gemma. You must think of our child. I've things to do here."

"Next time, I'll go to a doctor in Langley. I'm not comfortable with how people treat me knowing I'm with you."

His blood boiled. "No one treats my woman poorly. I'll make sure it doesn't happen again." He patted the hood of the car then strode away. Next time, Gemma had an appointment, he'd make sure she was the only one scheduled at that time. No one would be allowed to treat her with anything but respect.

He opened the glove compartment of the car Robert had driven and emptied it of the extra magazine clip then moved to the trunk where he withdrew a briefcase. The car would be admitted into evidence, and he didn't need his documents to be.

Quickly stashing them in his car, he headed to where the sheriff and Deputy O'Connor conversed. "Am I free to go?"

"Since you were not involved, yes." The sheriff barely glanced his way.

Insolence. "I sent the men that stopped those two from getting inside." Only two men to abduct Gemma? Was Esposito crazy?

"For that we are grateful. Excuse us, sir, we have work to do." The two men walked away.

Anthony stiffened. Something wasn't right. He'd sent the men that started a gunfight. Three men were dead. Why didn't the sheriff want to question him? He could understand if he'd given the sheriff a bribe to look the other way, but this didn't make sense.

He met the deputy's narrowed eyes. O'Connor was somehow behind the sheriff's actions.

~

"I could arrest him," Graham said, "but he'd only get off. We need to catch him in something solid. We'll find that something. I know we will."

The sheriff nodded. "But it galls me to see him walking around as a free man." He made a noise in his throat. "You're welcome, by the way."

"For what?' Graham tilted his head.

"Making you take your yearly checkup." His lip twitched. "If I hadn't, you wouldn't have been here to help keep those inside the clinic calm."

Graham laughed. "Thank you." The outcome could have been a lot worse if those two men had found a way inside. Knowing they were after Gemma frightened him more than anything. The danger toward her escalated, and he felt utterly helpless. "By the way, Gemma is carrying a boy."

"Which means Moreno will double down on claiming his empire now that he has a son to inherit." The sheriff shook his head. "I'm no longer a fan of waking up each morning. Every day is worse than the one before."

"When does our help arrive?"

"Sometime this afternoon. Go enjoy what's left of your day. I'll see you at work in the morning. I can handle cleaning this up."

Graham slid into his truck and pulled out the note from Gemma. "I am okay." Three little words that made him feel better. Not only because she was all right but because she cared enough to let him know.

Still feeling her arms around him, he started the truck and drove to the diner. Lucy would want to know that Gemma was safe. Word of the gunfight would have already reached the diner by now.

Lucy met him at the door. "My niece?"

"Safe. Moreno sent help." He sat at his usual table. "She's having a boy."

Lucy clapped her hands together. "Do you think Anthony will let me visit her since he keeps her in the house now?"

"Wouldn't hurt to try." This was his chance to get information from Gemma. "If he does, you can be the go-between. Pass on to me anything of value she tells you. I'm sure Gemma will insist Moreno allow you to visit if you bring up the subject."

"I'll go after work. Your lunch is on the house. The special is steak and eggs."

"I'll have that, and thank you."

Moreno entered the diner with Gemma. The man's lip curled, but he followed the hostess to a booth right behind his without saying anything.

Graham nodded a welcome as Moreno glanced his way. "This your celebration?"

"Don't be ridiculous. Gemma is hungry, and I promised to bring her to see her aunt." He slid into the same side of the booth as Gemma, effectively locking her in.

Lucy scurried over and slid in opposite them. "Thank you for bringing her. Graham told me the wonderful news. I'm wondering, Anthony, since you keep Gemma in the house for her safety, would it be all right for me to visit once or twice a week? I do miss her so."

Graham kept his ears trained on the conversation, praying the man would say yes.

After a few seconds of silence, Moreno answered, "Are you willing to visit with Gemma with Rosa around?"

"Absolutely."

"Do you mean it?" Gemma's voice rose with excitement. "This is a wonderful gift."

"I told you I wasn't an ogre. Just don't make me regret my decision. The occasional visit will help keep you occupied while I'm busy with work."

Graham grinned. If Gemma had to be in Moreno's clutches, at least now she could start searching for information again. Resources said that Moreno was rarely home, spending most of his time at the nightclub or the resort site.

Soon they'd have enough evidence to put him behind bars. He felt it in his gut.

Chapter Seventeen

Gemma hovered in the doorway of Anthony's office. Several times she raised her hand to knock only to drop her hand to her side. Would he believe her explanation? She needed to be there when he met with his people in order to gain any information at all.

She'd already scoured his office more than once and not found anything. Gemma needed to sneak into his office at the nightclub and the resort, if he had a place there yet.

One of Anthony's goons climbed the stairs, stopping at the sight of her. "Ma'am."

"I'll only be a minute." As if she hadn't been standing there debating, she rapped her knuckles against the carved wood, entering when Anthony said to come in. "Am I bothering you?"

He closed a folder and put his hands on the top. "Not at all." He smiled. "What brings me the pleasure?"

It wasn't an act to be frightened, but she merited a best-actress award if she pulled off wanting to go with him in order to build a stronger family. "I'm wondering whether I can go with you today? Be your shadow?"

He straightened and steepled his fingers. "What brings this on? Are you sure it's something you should do in your condition?"

She laughed. "It'll be easier than waitressing. For the sake of our family, I think it wise that I know the ins and outs of the business."

His brow furrowed. "That isn't something we do, Gemma. The women tend the homes, the men the business."

"Can't we change all that?" She perched on the counter of his desk and twirled her fingers around his tie. "Can I tag along? The supplies for the baby's room haven't arrived yet, and I'm bored." She paused for dramatic effect. "Or will your mistress mind?"

His eyes narrowed. "What makes you think I have one?"

"Oh, darling. I rejected you. Of course, you'd need to find comfort somewhere." She wanted to gag. "But, I'm back now."

He sighed and untangled her fingers. "I suppose it won't hurt for you to tag along for a day or two. However, you must do what I tell you when I tell you. Understood?"

"Absolutely." She tapped his cheek and strolled from the room. Mission one accomplished. Part two would be much harder, more dangerous.

In her room, she changed into comfortable shoes, capris, and a flowing blouse, then she grabbed her purse and went to collect Rosa. "We're sprung. Kind of. Can you follow my lead today?"

"Yes." She slipped the book she'd been reading into her bag. "I suspect you have something up that flowery sleeve."

"I do." Gemma grinned. "We're riding with Anthony today."

Rosa's eyes widened. "Isn't that dangerous?"

"Absolutely." She laughed and rushed to Anthony's waiting car.

Anthony sat up front with the driver, leaving the back seat to the women. Gemma settled into the buttery leather seats and was plotting her move when they reached their destination. She'd have to study the place in minute detail to find a flaw. *Get into the offices to flip through pages, get on the computer . . . all virtually impossible tasks.*

She stared out the window. Time was running out. Gemma placed her hands on her stomach. She had to help the authorities put Anthony behind bars. New York could worry about the senior Moreno. Misty Hollow needed her right now.

First stop, the nightclub. Good. She'd find out how Anthony managed to pull off the girls in the back.

He headed straight to his office but stopped and ordered the driver to stay in the main part of the club with the women, then he turned to Gemma. "Not quite sure what you can do while I work, but enjoy yourself."

"We'll be fine."

Gemma asked for a sparkling water from the bartender and settled into a corner table with Rosa. The driver lounged across the room and looked at his cell phone. Good. If his phone kept him entertained, he wouldn't be paying too much attention to her.

She pushed to her feet, shaking her head when Rosa made a move to follow. "Just going to stroll around. I'm not going anywhere." Gemma studied the walls and the women's restroom. Not finding anything other than security cameras placed in strategic places, nothing stood out to her. Wait. If Anthony wanted to let someone know to sound a warning, it would be a man, right?

Making sure Anthony's driver was still preoccupied, she ducked into the men's room. A red light had been mounted on the wall. She'd bet her favorite pair of shoes that it went off when someone entered the backrooms unescorted. Some poor fool was paid to hang out in the bathroom.

She peered out to make sure she hadn't been missed then strolled back to her table as if she hadn't made a wonderful discovery. "I need to get a message to Graham," she whispered.

"Here." Rosa pulled a small cell phone from inside her bra. Her lips twitched. "Burner phone. No one knows. Quick."

Gemma quickly typed out what she'd found in a text and pressed send. "You are a brave woman, Rosa." If Anthony discovered her deceit, she'd never be seen again.

"I don't trust the Morenos. Never have." She slipped the phone back into its hiding place and grinned. "Who's going to frisk an old woman?" Rosa cupped Gemma's cheek. "I accepted the hard-to-resist offer to help you."

"Thank you. Any ideas how to get into Anthony's office?"

"Forget that. It won't happen. Not unless we came back in the night after the place closes, and that is impossible." She leaned closer. "He keeps his most important papers in the trunk of his car. I saw him put some in yesterday."

All Gemma had to do was get ahold of his car keys. *Right.*

~

Graham showed Gemma's text to the sheriff.

"Looks like a couple of our borrowed hands will have to go undercover." He poured a cup of coffee and leaned against the breakroom counter. "Trigger the alarm and catch them coming out."

"Tonight?"

"As good a night as any." He grimaced and poured the coffee down the sink. "Someone needs to tell Doris how to make a good pot of coffee. Gather the others. We need to make sure everyone knows exactly what to do."

After an afternoon going over every detail of the night's raid, then grabbing a couple of hours rest, Graham now waited in the woods for word that the alarm had gone off inside. Then, he and the other deputies would storm the bar area.

"We're inside," Deputy Monroe said. "A couple of women are eyeing us. Time to play."

Graham shook his head. Two borrowed deputies from a neighboring county were now inside, undercover.

"Moreno's woman is here. Left side, corner table past the office. Has an old woman with her."

What was Gemma doing there? He thought she'd stopped going to the club at night.

"There are two men standing guard outside Moreno's office. Four more placed near each corner of the building. Since they stand out like a dog at a cat show, they're most likely security and armed. Hey, gorgeous." He turned off his mouthpiece.

Graham relaxed and prepared to wait.

Cars came and went in the parking lot. People stumbled from the club, while sober people went in. Others exited to smoke before going back in. The place sure didn't hurt for business.

"Where are you taking me, sweetheart?" Monroe

spoke again. "Well, this is nice."

"Do you always talk this much, cowboy?" A woman cooed.

Sheriff Westbrook motioned for Johnson and Young to enter through the same back door as they had for the unsuccessful raid. He then waved Graham to follow as he slowly made his way to the front doors. He raised his fist to halt. Now, they waited again.

"What's that alarm?" Monroe asked.

A female voice. "We have to go. Now. Act as if nothing happened." The rustling of clothes. "Quick."

"Back to the club? I didn't get what I paid for."

"You will. Later."

"Entering the club."

"We've got 'em." Sheriff Westbrook stepped into the open and barged through the front doors, Graham on his heels. "Everyone stay right where you are. No one leaves."

The two men guarding Moreno's door ducked into his office.

Graham darted forward. They'd locked the door behind them. From the other side, another door slammed. "Moreno is getting away!"

"Go after him." The sheriff drew his weapon as one of the guards near the restrooms drew his. "Don't do it." He dove to the floor and returned fire.

Graham dropped, trying to get a good look at Gemma as screaming women and men raced for the door. Monroe had a woman cuffed and shoved under the table. Same with the other undercover deputy. Now the two aimed weapons at guards as bullets continued to fly.

Graham scrambled in the direction of Gemma's table.

A guard stepped in front of him.

Graham's shot took the man in his knee.

He screamed, dropping his weapon.

Graham shoved it out of reach and continued his move toward Gemma.

He spotted her cowering under the table with Rosa and took up position in front of them. While none of Moreno's men would purposely harm Gemma, accidents happened, and there were a lot of wild bullets flying.

When the shots stopped, Graham stood and accessed the situation. Deputy Young clamped a hand over a wound in her arm. The two prostitutes were now seated at a table. Two guards lay dead, two injured.

He bent and held out his hand to Gemma. "You're safe now."

"Tell me it was worth it." She placed her hand in his and crawled from under the table. "Where's Anthony?"

"His men took him away."

Gemma huffed. "They treat him as if he's the president of the United States." She lowered onto a seat. "Hiding under there didn't help my back any."

He peered into her face. "Sweetheart, I have to go do my job. I'll make sure you get a ride home. Can you wait?"

"I'm sure that . . . oh, there's Nicco. My driver." A young Italian man stood in the doorway of the nightclub. Relief landed on his face at seeing Gemma. "See you around, Graham," she said softly. "Go put another nail in Anthony's business coffin." She linked arms with Rosa and headed for the door.

"It isn't much," Sheriff Westbrook said, "but we did at least stop the prostitution in this building. It won't get Moreno off the streets as fast as we'd like, I'm sure he'll go into hiding for a while, but it's something. Miss Ricca all right?"

"Yes. A little shook up, but she's protected as the mother of Moreno's child. It's the Espositos we have to worry about, not Moreno's men." He glanced over to see her led through the door.

If Moreno went into hiding, Gemma would have more freedom to dig into his affairs. Graham hated the thought that the department needed her in such a dangerous way.

~

"Gemma is in there." Anthony fought to free himself of the tight grip the guards had on him.

"We've called her driver to come get her. She will be fine." He opened the door to a dark sedan and shoved Anthony inside. "We need to get you to the safe house. There will be a warrant issued for your arrest."

He didn't care about that. They'd post bail, he'd pay, and he'd be out again. It happened on a regular basis. Still, his men would keep him hidden away for three days on orders from his father who considered it punishment for getting caught.

And it most certainly was the most excruciating sort of punishment. While hidden, Anthony had to rely on others to conduct his business. To watch over Gemma.

Someday, when he had more power than his father, the roles would be reversed. Anthony wouldn't be treated like a wayward child. His jaw tightened. With Gemma at his side, he could conquer the world and give it to his son.

Chapter Eighteen

The house seemed like a tomb with only Gemma, Rosa, and Nicco wandering the large Victorian. Where had they taken Anthony? How long would he be gone?

She gripped the keys to his car she'd nabbed from Nicco's nightstand. The man snored like a bear and hadn't stirred when she'd taken them.

With her heart in her throat, she padded barefoot downstairs and into the garage. She popped the trunk on the car Anthony usually rode in and stared at a briefcase. Could she be lucky enough to find what could put an end to the crime in Misty Hollow? The evidence that would put Anthony behind bars and secure her freedom?

She stared at the lock. She had no way to break into the case.

"Can I help you?" Nicco leaned against the doorjamb. "Only one person has the key to that case, and it's the boss."

She slipped her hand into the pocket of the loose pants she wore and turned on the recorder on her phone. "I want to know why someone tried to break into the clinic." It was as good a story as any.

"Because the boss killed Ricky Esposito on his

father's orders. Come back inside, Miss Ricca. You won't find anything to help you in the trunk."

She slammed it closed. "Anthony killed someone?"

"Uh-huh." His eyes narrowed. "He won't like you snooping around."

"I'm not snooping. I live here. We'll be getting married. I deserve to know what my husband-to-be is up to." She crossed her arms and looked as stern as she could muster while fighting back fear.

"That isn't how things are done."

"So, I've heard." She brushed past him. "Sorry to have disturbed you." Gemma dropped the keys on the kitchen counter. "You shouldn't sleep so soundly, Nicco. Someone could get in and harm us. Let's be quiet about this, all right? I'd hate for Anthony to know you were negligent." She turned from his astonished look and strode to her room.

Inside, she closed the door and leaned against it. She had no way of knowing whether she'd missed an opportunity or not. But she did have the recording. Gemma sent it via text to Graham and climbed into bed. Of course, Anthony would have taken anything important with him.

She stared at the ceiling. He probably had a bogus briefcase in each car. She couldn't be the only person who wanted what was inside. The Espositos would love to get their hands on anything that would give them an upper hand against the Morenos. Including her.

Something slammed against the house then exploded.

Gemma shrieked and glanced at the clock on her nightstand. Four a.m.

Another explosion sent her rolling from the bed and

cowering beside it.

"Come on." Nicco burst into the room. "I have to take you to the safe room."

"We have a safe room?" She snatched her phone and allowed him to take her arm, leading her downstairs to Anthony's office.

Inside, he tapped a book in the bookcase. The case slid to the side revealing a cement door. Nicco punched in a sequence of numbers and thrust her inside as the door opened.

"I'm here." Rosa bustled toward them. "I know you wouldn't have waited." She glared.

"Do not come out of there until I let you out." He hit a lever and the door closed, locking them into a darkness so thick Gemma couldn't see her hand in front of her face.

She turned on the flashlight on her phone and shined it around a room about ten-by-fifteen feet. Impressive. A panel of monitor screens lined one wall. Beneath them sat a desk and a computer.

Gemma powered up the computer. Immediately, she could see every room in the house plus the outdoors.

A car cruised past. Someone threw another explosive device at the house. Flames licked the post of the porch.

"Espositos," Rosa whispered. "They'll burn the place down around us."

"We'll be safe in here. See if you can find something to drink." Anything to keep her from hovering.

"There's a case of water, some champagne, other alcohol. They provided us snacks as well. Eat." She thrust a bottle of water and some trail mix at Gemma.

"I don't think we'll be in here long enough to need

all that." She watched as a van pulled up, and Anthony's men swarmed like bees.

The neighborhood erupted into another war.

The people of Misty Hollow were going to hate her if they didn't already. She sat in the desk chair and watched as warring men shot at each other.

Windows in the house shattered as the fire spread. Maybe they would be stuck in the safe room for a while.

Squad cars, sirens blazing, stopped behind the van. The sheriff, Graham, and others wearing armor poured out. Behind them waited an ambulance and fire truck.

"They'll need more ambulances." Rosa ate a granola bar. "Maybe they'll all kill themselves off."

"I haven't seen a single man fall. They're using cars as protection." Her gaze followed every movement Graham made as she prayed for his safety.

~

Graham stared at the burning house then, catching sight of Gemma's driver, raced over and spun the man to face him. "Miss Ricca?"

"In a safe room. The fire can't touch her." He shrugged him off and rejoined the fight.

"O'Connor!"

He turned to see the sheriff waving at him.

"Get back. We're tossing grenades."

Graham put down his face shield and took refuge behind a car as Johnson stepped forward with a firing cannon and let loose with a barrage of tear gas and pop grenades.

Shouts filled the air as gunshots ceased. Tires squealed as most of the fighters fled. One car careened out of control and slammed into a lamppost.

Sheriff Westbrook waved the fire truck forward.

"We've at least one inside locked in a safe room," Graham said.

"Must be nice to have the kind of money Moreno does." The sheriff headed for the house. "Find Gemma's driver. He won't have left with the others. She's his primary concern."

He spotted the driver in front of the house watching as firemen turned hoses on the flames.

"Nicco, where in the house?"

"The boss's office. I'll get her out when the fire is done." His tone dismissed Graham, but he would have nothing of it. He could arrest the man for what he'd heard on Gemma's recording, but the fact he'd saved her life made Graham hesitate.

Torn, he left Nicco to wait for Gemma and darted to the car that had hit the pole. One man dead, the other unconscious. "Medic!"

Two paramedics carrying a gurney rushed toward him. Graham left the surviving man in their capable hands and searched the other vehicles for victims. By now, people were stepping from their houses onto their porches and converging on the sidewalk, most in their pajamas and robes.

What a way to wake up. Would Misty Hollow ever be the same after this? If the fighting didn't stop, folks would flee in droves for safer pastures. The thought made his heart ache.

Commotion near the house drew his attention.

Nicco darted into what was left of the once beautiful home. The place could be saved, but it would take more than a bit to make it safe to live in. Where would Gemma go?

A few minutes later, Nicco reappeared with Gemma

and Rosa.

Graham rushed forward and wrapped Gemma in his arms. He rested his chin on her head not caring who saw. "Are you okay?"

"I'm fine, Graham." She pulled back and stared into his eyes. "Are you?"

He smiled. "Never better. Come away from here."

"I need to gather some things." She started to turn toward the house.

"Everything will have smoke and water damage, sweetheart." He took her hand and led her to the other side of the street. "Will you go to Lucy's?"

Her face paled. "There's nowhere safer for me than here, Graham." She shook her head. "Esposito won't stop until he has me. How can I stay safe?"

"I wish I could keep you safe." He pulled her close again, knowing he couldn't be what he yearned to be for her. Not until Moreno was out of the picture.

She sighed and rested her forehead on his chest. "I know."

"Miss Ricca. Where shall I take you?" Nicco curled his lip.

Gemma stepped free of Graham. "My aunt's house. I'm sure you'll send word to Anthony."

"Yes." He pulled his phone from his pocket and typed a message. "Ready?"

With one last glance at Graham, she followed the man to a waiting car.

"She's as safe as she can be." The sheriff stepped next to Graham. "We'll have a deputy drive by her aunt's home as often as possible. There's nothing more we can do short of putting her in protective custody."

"Which she won't do because Moreno will forbid

it." Graham wanted to curse but held back how he felt about the man safely squirreled away somewhere while the mother of his child dealt with war.

~

Anthony cursed and paced the floor of his prison, a mansion on the outskirts of Little Rock. Gemma and his child could have been killed, but his father refused to free him for another day at the least.

He'd make sure Nicco was handsomely rewarded for getting her into the safe room. What Anthony didn't like was the fact she'd be at Lucy's with no protection other than her driver and an old woman.

His thoughts drifted to Deputy O'Connor. Would he accept money to provide protection for his friend? Anthony scoffed, knowing full well the deputy cared more for Gemma than as a mere friend. That could also be a good thing. He'd do anything to keep her safe. The bad thing would be thrusting the two together.

No, he'd have to trust his men. That's what he paid them for. He'd join her as soon as possible, repair the house, and step up construction on the resort.

He called Nicco and asked to speak with Gemma. "Are you all right?"

"Yes. Nicco did very well." Her voice trembled. "We're headed to Lucy's. When are you returning?"

"As soon as my father feels I've suffered enough for what he believes is my failure." His grip tightened on the phone. "Possibly another day. Do I need to tell you not to go anywhere?"

"No. I can see the risk to my life and our child." Her voice chilled, no doubt blaming him for what was happening to her.

Not that he could blame her. He'd set a chain of

events into motion when he killed Ricky. A chain that could not be broken until the Espositos were finished.

"Be careful, my darling. I'll be home soon."

She hung up on him.

Someday, he'd make it all up to her. She'd live in luxury in a palace on top of the mountain where she could look down on all those who would willingly serve her. Who needed a penthouse in New York when they could have an entire valley?

Yes, everyone would do her bidding or suffer. Anthony wasn't his father's son for nothing. He knew the power he and his family could wield.

His first deed once his plan reached fruition would be to get rid of the local law enforcement and fill the department with men he could buy. He chuckled. That meant getting rid of Deputy O'Connor.

Chapter Nineteen

Seated in Lucy's kitchen, Gemma and Lucy ate a simple breakfast of biscuits and chocolate gravy, something Gemma had never had. "This is wonderful," she said.

"A southern favorite." Worry creased her aunt's brow. "It worries me that Anthony has been gone for so long. You'd think his father would care more about his grandchild. You're safest when Anthony is near."

"Moreno Senior trusts me to fill in." Nicco entered the kitchen and stared at the pan of gravy. He shrugged and fixed himself a plate.

Lucy cut him a glare. "You're a hired minion not a Moreno."

"The son is being punished by the father," Rosa said. "It's the way they do things. He'll be here today."

"How do you know that?" Nicco's eyes narrowed.

"You left your phone on the table when you went to the bathroom." She grinned. "It wasn't locked. Big mistake."

"I should kill you for that."

She shrugged. "Anthony will not be pleased if you do."

"One thing you don't know is that he plans on wedding Miss Ricca as soon as he returns. Doesn't want his son born on the wrong side of the bed."

Gemma's eyes widened. "Say I don't?"

"You'll never see your child once it's born."

A knock sounded on the door.

Hand on the gun at his hip, Nicco went to answer. "It's the deputy," he snarled, letting Graham in.

"Just checking on Gemma." His eyes landed on her. "You okay?"

"Yes, please, join us for breakfast. It's chocolate gravy."

"Can't refuse that." Graham flashed Nicco a grin and took a seat.

"The boss is coming back today." Nicco resumed his seat. "He won't be pleased to see you here."

"I'll be gone by then."

Gemma's face flushed under Graham's warm gaze. She wished he could stay. How different life with him would be compared to one with Anthony. Marrying a Moreno meant a life of crime and danger. Somehow, she needed to find a way out. For her sake and the baby's.

She gasped as her son dealt her a hard kick. Only a month more, my child. The thought both thrilled her and cast a cloud of despair over her head. She sent Graham an imploring look. Oh, how she wished he could save her from her fate.

He reached over and put his hand over hers. "Are you sure you're all right?"

Tears sprang from her eyes. She ducked her head, hoping he wouldn't see. "I will be fine. It's a little too much is all."

"It'll be over soon. I promise."

She jerked her gaze back to his. "Don't make promises you can't keep." Nothing would be all right once she married Anthony.

Graham leaned close and whispered, "Should I kiss you now?"

Gemma bit back a grin and shoved him away. "Behave." She was going to miss him so much. Being friends would not be allowed once she became Mrs. Moreno.

Graham finished his breakfast. "Delicious as always, Lucy. I've missed eating with the two most beautiful women in town." He stood behind Nicco and blew kisses at Gemma.

Her face heated, and she suppressed a giggle. What a nut he could be.

The sun left with him as the front door closed. Gemma moved to the window to watch as he slid into his car and drove away. She put her hand on the glass. "Goodbye, Graham."

Once he had gone out of sight, she helped clear the table while Nicco moved to the living room to watch a sports game. Table cleared, Gemma filled the sink with hot soapy water.

"I will do that." Rosa nudged her away. "Go sit. I see weariness is heavy on you."

"I need to stay busy."

"She's right, Gemma. Go relax. Rosa and I will do the dishes." Lucy took her by the shoulders and nudged her toward the door. "Read a book or something."

She chose a mystery from her aunt's bookshelf and settled onto the sofa to read. Hopefully, the story would transport her away from her problems.

The front door banged open. Two armed men

barged inside.

Gemma tossed the book aside and raced for the bedroom as shots rang out. Her hand gripped the doorknob when one of the shooters grabbed her. No amount of kicking and screaming freed her. He dragged her toward the front door.

"No!" She choked back a sob at the sight of Rosa and Lucy lying in pools of blood in the kitchen. Nicco lay on the living room floor. Graham, where are you? *Please, God, don't let them get to him.*

Both men held her by the arms and forced her into a waiting van. Neither of them spoke as the van sped away from her aunt's house.

Gemma huddled in the corner, arms wrapped protectively around her middle, and cried.

~

Anthony froze at the sight of the open door. His heart dropped as he sprinted inside. "Gemma!"

He scanned the bodies, relieved not to find her among them. After searching the house, he called his father. "They got her. Nicco, the nanny, and the aunt are dead."

"Are you sure?"

"That they're dead? I'm not touching them. I don't want any sign of me being here." His hands were already stained with Ricky Esposito's blood. He rushed back to his car, putting his father on speaker before speeding away from the house. "Where would the Espositos take her?"

"Where are they holed up? Think, son!"

"What I think is that this wouldn't have happened if you hadn't locked me up." He did something he'd never done. Hung up on his father. When the phone rang again, he ignored it. Instead, he rallied his men together and told them to meet him at the club.

There would not be a single Esposito alive by the end of the day. Most of his men arrived at the club before he did. He gathered them in the bar area. "Where is Esposito?"

"In Langley. They've rented an entire motel." The bartender tossed a towel in the sink. "Heard someone mentioning it the other day. Figured you knew."

Someone had dropped the ball on that, and Anthony was not pleased. "Arm yourselves. We're rescuing my future wife back at any cost." If they harmed her, their deaths would not be painless or quick.

A line of black SUVs left the nightclub. Anthony rode in the first one. He wanted to shoot the first bullet. Anthony had to be the one that rid the world of the senior Esposito.

The vehicles parked behind those in front of the motel, blocking any possible retreat. Leading the pack, Anthony clutched his gun and strode to the manager's office.

"You work for Esposito?" He aimed the gun at the frightened old man.

"No, sir. Just rented the rooms."

"Then go. You don't want to be here for this." Anthony stepped back outside where his men waited. "Go room to room, shooting everyone you see. Find Gemma."

Anthony kicked in the first door and shot the man reclining on the bed. He didn't waste time asking for names. If they were in the hotel, they worked for Esposito.

Most of the rooms were empty. One lavishly

decorated room had to belong to Esposito Senior. Anthony found no sign of Gemma.

Where could they have taken her?

~

After hearing a report on shots fired at Lucy's residence, Graham and Joey made haste. Graham burst inside. "Gemma?"

He spotted Rosa and Lucy in the kitchen and knelt to check for life. He detected a faint pulse in Lucy. Rosa was dead. "Call for an ambulance. Lucy is alive."

"The driver isn't," Joey said.

Graham straightened, then searched the house, knowing he wouldn't find Gemma. She'd been taken.

"Lots of gunfire at a motel in Langley," Joey said. "I'll take care of this. You go."

Graham sprinted for his car. He'd never make it in time to prevent further death. His only hope was that Gemma wasn't there.

Sirens wailing and lights flashing, he sped the thirty miles to Langley making it in record time. A call to Doris told him which motel.

Graham pulled into the lot as several SUVS were pulling out. He slammed the car into park and climbed out. "Moreno!"

One SUV stopped, and the man got out, waving the others to continue before turning to Graham. "Deputy."

"Where's Gemma?"

"Esposito has her. He hasn't contacted me yet. I thought he would be here."

"What have you done?"

"Left a message." His features hardened. "If you know where he might have taken her, Deputy, now is the time to tell me."

"I have no idea." He glanced at the waiting SUV. "I'm going to have to arrest you, sir."

"If you try, my man inside will shoot you. As close as he is, the shot will be fatal. You can't find Gemma if you're dead." He marched back to the vehicle. "Esposito should pray you find him first. That's the only way he'll walk away from this." He climbed into the back seat, and the vehicle drove away.

Graham stared after it, stunned at the course of events. Everything had happened in such a short time—mere hours since breakfast.

Several squad cars pulled into the lot as the Langley police department arrived. One of them approached Graham.

He showed his identification. "I thought an abducted woman would be here. She isn't. I haven't searched any of the rooms, but several vehicles were pulling away as I arrived."

"Then she could be here."

Graham shook his head. "No. She's too valuable to be killed. At least, right now. What I'm hoping you can tell me is where Richard Esposito might be. Where would he take a hostage?"

"Does this have something to do with all the trouble you folks in Misty Hollow are having? We've sent several officers your way to help."

"It has everything to do with that trouble."

"I'm sorry, Deputy, but I have no idea where the man you're looking for could be. We do have one hotel he might find suitable for his tastes." He gave Graham the name and directions.

"Thanks." Graham got back into his car.

His phone rang. He glanced at the screen and

grimaced. "Yes, sir."

"Get back here. You can't go after Esposito alone," the sheriff said. "We'll send men with you."

"But, sir—"

"You run off like some hero cowboy and I'll have your badge." The sheriff hung up.

Graham felt torn between rushing to where Gemma might be and following orders. He decided to follow orders, despite his heart's reluctance. He couldn't help her if he was killed. The sheriff was right. He needed backup.

Graham headed into the sheriff's office expecting a lecture. Instead, the sheriff barely spared him a glance.

"We're meeting in the conference room. Tell me you know where Miss Ricca is."

"I do." He gave the name of the hotel. "No confirmation that she is there, just the local police's suspicions."

"Works for me." The sheriff led him to the conference room where the other deputies and borrowed police officers waited. "Lucy is in the hospital. She's lost a lot of blood but is expected to make a full recovery."

"That's great news." He knew how much she meant to Gemma. Rather than take a seat, Graham paced the room while the sheriff went over the details and each person's role.

"We don't want any heroes." He shot Graham a sharp look. "We can't help Miss Ricca if she's caught in the crossfire. It's a large hotel. We'll need to search every room without Richard Esposito catching wind. It won't be easy. And that's if he's even there."

He had to be. Sweat trickled down Graham's back. What would the man do to Gemma? How long would he keep her alive before taking revenge for his son's death? Was Gemma the one the man wanted, or was she simply the bait to get to Anthony Moreno?

Chapter Twenty

They drove Gemma to a ritzy hotel in Langley—at least ritzy for that part of the country—and thrust her into a chair. No one spoke to her; no one looked at her. Her two captors sat in chairs across the room and dug into a tray of food that looked like something room service would have brought up.

She squirmed, her back aching from the rough ride in the van. Her eyes studied the room for a way to escape, a weapon—anything.

Two queen beds, a sofa bed, small kitchenette—everything a person needed to stay for a while. Well, she didn't intend to stay for any length of time; she would find a way out.

How could she have been so stupid, so blind as to ignore the warning signs of what the Morenos did? Their name was well-known in New York by the rich and poor. Gemma covered her face with her hands. She'd known deep down they were part of organized crime plaguing the city. Why hadn't she been brave enough at the beginning?

Answer: Because Anthony had started pursuing her in college and wouldn't stop. She could see it now. His obsession had frightened her at the same time as making her feel special that a man as handsome as Anthony Moreno would want her. The boarding school in which she'd spent her teen years had not prepared her to fight off his advances. She'd chosen, freely chosen, to become the fiancée of a known criminal.

A sob escaped. It was her fault Rosa and Lucy were dead. If she would've followed her conscience all those years ago . . . no, she'd berate herself later. Right now, she had to find a way out of here. She shifted on the seat again, standing when she couldn't find relief for her aching back.

One of the men peered up with narrowed eyes. "Where do you think you're going? Sit down. The boss is on his way."

"To the bathroom." She hitched her chin. "Unless you want to deprive a pregnant woman of using the restroom."

The goon shrugged. "Go ahead. You can't get out that way." He laughed and glanced at his friend. "She won't need such basic conveniences for long."

Their laughter sent an icy trickle down her spine as she closed and locked the bathroom door. She leaned against it. The man was right. There was no way out.

Still, she held onto hope. Esposito wouldn't kill her in the hotel. Too many people. She'd have to make a run for it when they transported her somewhere else.

Gemma splashed cold water on her face then dried herself with the hand towel near the sink. Something fell to the floor. She glanced down and smiled. A cheap razor. She turned the faucet on full blast to hide the sound of her crushing the plastic of the razor with her foot, then carefully slipped the razor blade into her pocket. She'd chance a few scratches to have a weapon.

Squaring her shoulders, she opened the door and took a seat on the sofa instead of the hard chair and did her best to act as if she wasn't afraid for her life. Again, the men ignored her, so she turned on the television and watched a cooking show. All she had to do was stay alive long enough for Graham to find her. He wouldn't stop until he did—she knew that for a fact. Neither would Anthony.

The room phone rang. One of the men answered then peered at Gemma. "We'll be right there." He glanced at his buddy. "You want to take her or shall I?"

"Go ahead. I'm not finished eating."

Her escort grabbed her by the arm and hauled her to her feet. "Looks like it's just me and you, little lady."

Gemma winced as another sharp pain shot through her back. "Oh, goody." She tried to pull free only to have his grip tighten.

"Come on. I don't like babysitting." He led her into the hall and toward the elevator.

The instant they turned the corner out of sight of the room, Gemma pulled the blade from her pocket and sliced the hand holding her arm. Before the man could react, she slashed at his face then pushed the button for the elevator.

He howled and fell back against the wall.

She jumped into the elevator and frantically pushed the button to close the doors.

"I hope I get to watch you die," he roared, blood seeping through his fingers.

The door closed, and she pushed the button for the bottom floor. She'd done it. Almost free.

The elevator seemed to take a long time to reach the bottom level despite it not stopping at every floor. Good.

Gemma didn't want anyone else involved. This was her fight.

She groaned and arched her back. Her stomach felt ten times heavier than it had earlier that day.

The doors slid open. She peered out to see several Esposito men in the common area. As quickly as she could, shoving aside the pain that standing produced, she rushed out of the elevator and entered the kitchen.

It wasn't until she saw the shocked looks on the staff's faces that she realized her hand and arm were covered in Esposito's goon's blood. "A towel, please?"

A young woman rushed to the commercial stainless-steel sink and soaked a rag. "Are you injured?"

"No." Gemma wiped the blood from her arm. "I'm fine. Ow!" She doubled over and clutched her stomach.

Her water broke as gunfire erupted outside the kitchen.

She met the startled faces of the staff who froze for just a second then ran.

Gemma searched for a place to hide. She'd never make it by running. Not with her baby deciding to make an early entrance to the world.

Spotting a large door, she stepped inside the kitchen pantry and closed the door behind her. Her breath came in gasps. This was not where she wanted to give birth. She groaned and lowered herself to the floor and prayed.

~

"Find Gemma!" Anthony waved his men forward. "Shoot anyone that gets in your way, but leave Esposito to me." He headed for the elevator, wrinkling his nose at the smear of blood on the button panel. Using the barrel of his gun, he pressed the button for the top floor knowing Esposito was just like him. They needed to be on top.

The doors opened and the sound of gunfire in the distance spurred Anthony toward the door at the end of the hall. A quick bullet between the eyes of the man standing guard, then he entered the room.

Esposito sat on a white leather sofa and arched a brow. "I don't recall inviting you here."

"Where is the mother of my child?"

"That's right. She ditched you at the altar, didn't she? Care for a drink?" He motioned to a whiskey decanter.

"Where is she?"

"I have no idea. She attacked my man and fled. I suppose she's holed up like a frightened mouse somewhere in this hotel. I do hope a stray bullet doesn't find her." He laughed. "Of course, that would mean your only son is also dead. A shame that it couldn't be by my hand." He downed the liquid in the crystal glass he held. "What now? An old-fashioned shootout? Count off the paces and turn?" He chuckled. "You have a lot to learn, young Moreno. Do you truly think that I would be here in my room alone?" He snapped his fingers.

The first shot spun Anthony around to face the shooter. The second shot dropped him. His eyes closed to the sound of Esposito's laughter and the order to drag him into the hall with the other garbage.

~

Graham darted past the pool and through the back door of the hotel.

A young woman grabbed his arm. "There's a pregnant woman in the kitchen. I think she's having a baby."

The words were barely out of her mouth before he

made a mad dash for the kitchen. Hold on, baby. I'm coming.

He burst through the swinging double doors. "Gemma!"

"Graham! Hurry."

He searched the room. When she called out again, he flung open the door to the pantry and fell to his knees beside her.

She gripped his shirt. "The baby is coming, Graham. It's too early."

"I'll call you an ambulance."

Her hold tightened. "Don't leave me." Tears streamed down her face.

"Never." He cupped her cheek then pulled his phone from his pocket and told the sheriff where he was. When he hung up, he asked, "Do you think the baby will wait until you reach the hospital?"

"I don't think the baby will come on its own. Something doesn't feel right." She groaned and fell back.

It didn't take more than a couple of minutes for two paramedics to enter the kitchen and order him to move out of the way. They lifted Gemma onto a gurney and wheeled her outside to a waiting ambulance.

The shooting had stopped. Bodies of both Moreno men and Esposito men littered the ground, most still alive but wounded.

Graham caught sight of Anthony Moreno being lifted into another ambulance. He waved the sheriff over. "Is Moreno dead?"

"Not yet, but it doesn't look good. Miss Ricca?"

"In full labor." He set his jaw. "I'm going to the hospital with her." He climbed into the ambulance.

The sheriff nodded. "I'll see you later. Keep me

informed."

"I will." Graham moved to Gemma's side and took her hand. "We'll do this together, sweetheart."

Her wide eyes focused on his. "Promise?"

"I do." He prayed it was a promise he could keep. What if she lost the baby due to the stress of the last few days? It would wreck her. He brought her hand to his lips. What if he ended up losing her?

At the hospital, a nurse stopped him on the maternity ward. "Are you the father?"

"No, but—"

"Then wait out here, sir."

"No." Gemma stretched out a hand. "I need him with me. Please."

The nurse searched Graham's face. "All right, but stay out of the way."

He'd do anything they told him as long as he could stay with her. In the room, he stayed in the corner, his heart in his throat as nurses and a doctor checked Gemma and the baby.

"Going to need an emergency C-section," the doctor said. "This baby wants out, but the mother isn't ready." He put a hand on Gemma's shoulder. "Everything will be fine, Miss Ricca."

A nurse put a mask on her face while another inserted an IV. "Count backward from ten, Miss Ricca."

Gemma's eyes drifted closed.

Graham couldn't bear the sight of them cutting open the woman he loved, but he couldn't look away. He'd promised not to leave her. That meant keeping his gaze on her face. He didn't know how long it took, but it seemed like only a breath or two before the doctor held up a baby boy who squalled like a cat whose tail had been stepped on. Graham rushed forward as a nurse placed the baby on Gemma's chest and removed her mask.

Her eyes flickered open to rest on Graham then on her son. Her lips curved into a smile. "We did it."

Laughing, Graham ran the back of his finger down the baby's soft cheek. "Yes, you did." His heart swelled with love for both her and her child.

"What about Anthony?" She asked.

"He's been shot. Anthony's here in the hospital. So is Lucy."

"She's alive?" Hope lit up her face.

"Going to be just fine." Graham smiled then sobered. "Anthony isn't expected to pull through."

She pressed her lips into a thin line. "Then, I'll need to take his son to him. Will you go with me?"

"As soon as the doctor says it's okay."

Chapter Twenty-One

Graham settled Gemma into a wheelchair, and the nurse handed her the baby. "Does he have a name?" She asked.

"Not yet." Gemma smiled at her child despite the sadness in her heart. She'd wanted free of the Morenos but not in this way. Would Anthony's father come for his grandchild? Would she ever be free of them?

"Are you sure you're up to this?" Graham gripped the handles of the wheelchair.

"He should have the opportunity to see his son." She glanced over her shoulder. "You said he isn't expected to live."

Graham's face fell. "No, he isn't."

"Then . . . okay." She took a deep breath.

Despite the severity of his injuries, Anthony's room was heavily guarded. The two officers simply nodded as Graham wheeled Gemma inside his room and up to the bed.

"Anthony?" Gemma patted his shoulder. "Open your eyes and see your son."

His eyes barely opened. He reached out, his hand trembling, and laid it on his swaddled son. "What will you name him?"

"Angelo. It means angel of God."

A tear trickled down his cheek. "It's perfect." His gaze rose to Gemma's. "I'm sorry. Please, forgive me."

"I do. You're a product of your lifestyle, Anthony." She patted his hand. "But, I don't want that for my child."

"I know. I've got to go now." His eyes drifted closed. "I do love you, Gemma." His chest rose and fell, then rose and fell, not to rise again.

Gemma raised his hand to her cheek then placed it at his side. "I'm ready." She glanced up, surprised and touched that Graham had let her say goodbye in peace. "Graham?"

"I'm here." He smiled. "You okay?"

She nodded. "He's gone. Someone will need to tell his father."

"That isn't your job. Sheriff Westbrook will take care of it or the doctor." He wheeled her from the room and back to her bed. Graham helped her settle in then lifted Angelo and placed the baby in his bassinet. "The baby's beautiful."

"I've named him Angelo Anthony. I don't want him to have the last name Moreno, so I guess he's a Ricca." She plucked at the blanket over her legs.

Graham took her hand. "Let me take care of you and the baby. I love you, Gemma. Let's find out what the future holds for us. Together. He can be Angelo Anthony O'Connor." He laughed. "Irish Italian. Lord help the world."

"This child will always be a Moreno." Her gaze searched his, hoping to find what he promised.

"But he won't be raised as one." He took her hand. "I already love him, Gemma. I'll be a good father."

She knew he would. Graham would be the best father. "What about Moreno Senior?"

"We'll deal with him when and if we have to." His eyes crinkled. "Say yes and let me finally get that kiss I've been hungering for."

She laughed. "Yes, I will be your Mrs. O'Connor." The broken pieces of her heart fell into place. "Now, kiss me."

He obliged with the sweetest kiss she'd ever received.

"Now, I'm going to do something very inappropriate." He pulled back the blanket. "I'm exhausted, and there is only one bed. Let me fall asleep holding you."

"The nurse will run you off." She grinned, scooting over.

"Let her try." He stretched out beside her, his large body taking up most of the space. His arm snaked around her. "Let me know if I'm hurting you."

"Shut up and kiss me again."

The End

Dear Reader,

I hope you're enjoying the romance and suspense of Misty Hollow where real people deal with real circumstances . . . well, where real people with real emotions and life issues are thrust into extraordinary circumstances. If you enjoyed *Say I Don't*, please visit Amazon and leave a review. Reviews are the lifeblood for an author.

Stay tuned for the next book, *A Place to Hide*.

God Bless,

Cynthia Hickey

www.cynthiahickey.com

Cynthia Hickey is a multi-published and best-selling author of cozy mysteries and romantic suspense. She has taught writing at many conferences and small writing retreats. She and her husband run the publishing press, Winged Publications, which includes some of the CBA's best well-known authors. They live in Arizona and Arkansas, becoming snowbirds with two dogs and one cat. They have ten grandchildren who keep them busy and tell everyone they know that "Nana is a writer."

Connect with me on FaceBook
Twitter
Sign up for my newsletter and receive a free short story
www.cynthiahickey.com

Follow me on Amazon
And Bookbub

Enjoy other books by Cynthia Hickey

Misty Hollow
Secrets of Misty Hollow
Deceptive Peace
Calm Surface
Lightning Never Strikes Twice
Lethal Inheritance

Bitter Isolation
Say I Don't

The Tail Waggin' Mysteries
Cat-Eyed Witness
The Dog Who Found a Body
Troublesome Twosome
Four-Legged Suspect
Unwanted Christmas Guest
Wedding Day Cat Burglar

Brothers Steele
Sharp as Steele
Carved in Steele
Forged in Steele
Brothers Steele (All three in one)

The Brothers of Copper Pass
Wyatt's Warrant
Dirk's Defense
Stetson's Secret
Houston's Hope
Dallas's Dare
Seth's Sacrifice
Malcolm's Misunderstanding
The Brothers of Copper Pass Boxed Set

Time Travel
The Portal

Tiny House Mysteries

No Small Caper
Caper Goes Missing
Caper Finds a Clue
Caper's Dark Adventure
A Strange Game for Caper
Caper Steals Christmas
Caper Finds a Treasure
Tiny House Mysteries boxed set

Wife for Hire – Private Investigators
Saving Sarah
Lesson for Lacey
Mission for Meghan
Long Way for Lainie
Aimed at Amy
Wife for Hire (all five in one)

A Hollywood Murder
Killer Pose, book 1
Killer Snapshot, book 2
Shoot to Kill, book 3
Kodak Kill Shot, book 4
To Snap a Killer
Hollywood Murder Mysteries

Shady Acres Mysteries
Beware the Orchids, book 1
Path to Nowhere
Poison Foliage
Poinsettia Madness
Deadly Greenhouse Gases
Vine Entrapment

Shady Acres Boxed Set

CLEAN BUT GRITTY Romantic Suspense

Highland Springs

Murder Live
Say Bye to Mommy
To Breathe Again
Highland Springs Murders (all 3 in one)

Colors of Evil Series

Shades of Crimson
Coral Shadows

The Pretty Must Die Series

Ripped in Red, book 1
Pierced in Pink, book 2
Wounded in White, book 3
Worthy, The Complete Story

Lisa Paxton Mystery Series

Eenie Meenie Miny Mo
Jack Be Nimble
Hickory Dickory Dock
Boxed Set

Hearts of Courage
A Heart of Valor

The Game
Suspicious Minds
After the Storm
Local Betrayal
Hearts of Courage Boxed Set

Overcoming Evil series
Mistaken Assassin
Captured Innocence
Mountain of Fear
Exposure at Sea
A Secret to Die for
Collision Course
Romantic Suspense of 5 books in 1

INSPIRATIONAL

Nosy Neighbor Series
Anything For A Mystery, Book 1
A Killer Plot, Book 2
Skin Care Can Be Murder, Book 3
Death By Baking, Book 4
Jogging Is Bad For Your Health, Book 5
Poison Bubbles, Book 6
A Good Party Can Kill You, Book 7
Nosy Neighbor collection

Christmas with Stormi Nelson

The Summer Meadows Series
Fudge-Laced Felonies, Book 1

Candy-Coated Secrets, Book 2
Chocolate-Covered Crime, Book 3
Maui Macadamia Madness, Book 4
All four novels in one collection

The River Valley Mystery Series
Deadly Neighbors, Book 1
Advance Notice, Book 2
The Librarian's Last Chapter, Book 3
All three novels in one collection

Historical cozy
Hazel's Quest

Historical Romances
Runaway Sue
Taming the Sheriff
Sweet Apple Blossom
A Doctor's Agreement
A Lady Maid's Honor
A Touch of Sugar
Love Over Par
Heart of the Emerald
A Sketch of Gold
Her Lonely Heart

Finding Love the Harvey Girl Way
Cooking With Love
Guiding With Love
Serving With Love

Warring With Love
All 4 in 1

Finding Love in Disaster
The Rancher's Dilemma
The Teacher's Rescue
The Soldier's Redemption

Woman of courage Series

A Love For Delicious
Ruth's Redemption
Charity's Gold Rush
Mountain Redemption
They Call Her Mrs. Sheriff
Woman of Courage series

Short Story Westerns
Desert Rose
Desert Lilly
Desert Belle
Desert Daisy
Flowers of the Desert 4 in 1

Contemporary

Romance in Paradise
Maui Magic
Sunset Kisses
Deep Sea Love
3 in 1

Finding a Way Home
Service of Love
Hillbilly Cinderella
Unraveling Love
I'd Rather Kiss My Horse

Christmas
Dear Jillian
Romancing the Fabulous Cooper Brothers
Handcarved Christmas
The Payback Bride
Curtain Calls and Christmas Wishes
Christmas Gold
A Christmas Stamp
Snowflake Kisses
Merry's Secret Santa
A Christmas Deception

The Red Hat's Club (Contemporary novellas)

Finally
Suddenly
Surprisingly
The Red Hat's Club 3 – in 1

Short Story

One Hour (A short story thriller)
Whisper Sweet Nothings (a Valentine short romance)

SAY I DON'T

www.ingramcontent.com/pod-product-compliance
Lightning Source LLC
Chambersburg PA
CBHW070507200726
48293CB00007B/2429